Tomahawk Entertainment Group Presents:

Common Creed: The Epidemic

Javon Bates

ISBN: 10: 0-692-17966-6
ISBN-13: 13: 978-0-692-17966-6

DEDICATION

This is dedicated to all the people in the world working on their dreams and goals. Keep working hard and stay consistently in action. Also to the families struggling with love ones who have drug addictions, get help, get better and take one day at a time.

CONTENTS

This book is based on information from the Opioid epidemic in Ohio as well as in America. These are true events installed behind each chapter. This epidemic can cost you your life as well as prison time being served. It might seem like easy money but sometimes your greed opens other evil doors. These wide-ranging events occur often and prevalent, surviving is what we all believe in morally or dishonorably.

This is Common Creed……..

Dangerous and deadly: Warning!! Can cause death, prison sentences and destruction upon others

The Education of the epidemic-Common Creed

The Opioid Epidemic rapid increase in the use of prescription and non-prescription **opioid** drugs in the **United States** and **Canada** beginning in the late 1990s and continuing throughout the next two decades. Opioids are a diverse class of moderately strong **painkillers**, including **oxycodone** (commonly sold under the trade names **OxyContin** and **Percocet**), **hydrocodone** (**Vicodin**), and a very strong painkiller, **fentanyl**, which is synthesized to resemble other **opiates** such as **opium**-derived **morphine** and **heroin**.

The potency and availability of these substances, despite their high risk of **addiction** and **overdose**, have made them popular both as formal medical treatments and as **recreational drugs**. Due to their **sedative** effects on the part of the brain which regulates breathing, the **respiratory center** of the **medulla oblongata**, opioids in high doses present the potential for **respiratory depression**, and may cause **respiratory failure** and **death**.

Fentanyl is a painkiller commonly used by drug dealers to cut heroin. The drug's potency is 10,000 times more powerful than morphine.

Fentanyl can cause a person to overdose through skin contact.

By The Numbers

Ohio's opiate epidemic is a crisis

of unparalleled proportions with devastating, often

deadly, consequences. Opiates include both heroin and

prescription pain reliever medications. In fact, these

substances accounted for nearly 63 percent of the state's

1,544 overdose deaths in 2010. In addition to the human

toll, Ohio's opiate and prescription drug epidemic has

severely strained law enforcement, criminal justice and

health care resources and stretched the capacity of Ohio's

publicly-funded alcohol and other drug addiction

treatment services system.

Southern Ohio has been particularly hard-hit by this crisis

and is widely considered "a window on the world" in

terms of the wreckage caused when prescription drug

abuse and addiction becomes entrenched in a community.

The Ohio State Board of Pharmacy reported 8.2 million

doses were legally dispensed to Scioto County residents

in 2011. This is double the per capital rate dispensed in

Cuyahoga County (Greater Cleveland). Scioto County, which has less than 79,000 residents, had the highest overdose death rate (26.0) per 100,000 from 2006-2010. On average, four Ohioans die each day as a result of drug overdose since 2016. If all the junkies in Ohio lived in one place it would be the 5th largest city in the state. There are reported over 200,000 opioid addicts statewide. That would be the size of the city of Akron, Ohio. In the last 2 years statewide 4,000 babies have been treated for neonatal abstinence syndrome. The syndrome affects babies born to mothers who are addicted to opioids. They are going through withdrawal as they are born. Ohio leads the nation in opioid-related emergency room visits. In 2016, Cleveland Clinic reported more than 2,300 opioid-related ED visits, including 1,200 overdoses.

The prescription opioids most often found responsible mirror national statistics:

- Oxycodone, the generic name for OxyCotin

- Hydrocodone, the generic name for Vicodin

- Methadone, a synthetic opioid used in heroin addiction treatment

- Fentanyl, typically found in patch (transdermal) form

- Morphine

Police busted a fentanyl ring in Columbus,Ohio found enough of the drug to kill the population of the entire city. Investigators ended up finding 4.5 pounds of fentanyl in that drug bust in October of 2017, which could have wiped out the city of about 800,00 residents.

Ohio has 11.6 million residents and. At 2 to 3 milligrams per lethal dose, the amount of fentanyl discovered in November 2017 bust could have potentially kill more than 9 million people.

Two or three milligrams of fentanyl is not much more than five or six grains of salt.

But the epidemic goes beyond Ohio. Some of the major opioid busts this year could have killed the entire populations of several states.

Heroin Trafficking

In the state of Ohio, drug trafficking is defined as selling, offering, or packaging for delivery a "controlled substance," as stipulated by the Ohio Revised Code. "Controlled substances" are classified under five schedules, with I being the most severe and V being the least severe. The severity of a heroin trafficking conviction is based on the amount of heroin found.

Different amounts with corresponding convictions are detailed below.

up to 1 gram: 5th degree felony (6-12 months)

1 – <5 grams: 4th degree felony (6-18 months)

5 – <10 grams: 3rd degree felony, presumption in favor of prison time (9 months – 3 years)

10 – 50 grams: 2nd degree felony, prison time mandatory (2 - 8years)

50 – <250 grams: 1st degree felony, prison time mandatory (3-10 years)

≥250 grams: Major drug offense (MDO), maximum prison time (11 year

<u>Heroin Possession</u>

If you are caught in possession of heroin in the state of Ohio, you can face thousands of dollars in penalties and up to a decade in prison. See the information below for a quick breakdown of heroin possession penalties based on amount.

Up to 1 gram: 5th degree felony, 6-12 months in prison (in favor of community control)

1 to < 5 gram: 4th degree felony, 6-18 months in prison (in favor of community control)

5 to < 10 grams: 3rd degree felony, 9 months to 3 years in prison (in favor of community control)

10 to < 50 grams: 2nd degree felony, 2-8 years in prison (mandatory).

50 to <250 grams: 1st degree felony, 3-10 years in prison (mandatory).

250 grams or more: Major drug offense (MDO), 11 years in prison (mandatory).

The Opioid Epidemic rapid increase in the use of prescription and non-prescription opioid drugs in the United States and Canada beginning in the late 1990s and continuing throughout the next two decades. Opioids are a diverse class of moderately strong painkillers, including oxycodone (commonly sold under the trade names OxyContin and Percocet), hydrocodone (Vicodin), and a very strong painkiller, fentanyl, which is synthesized to resemble other opiates such as opium-derived morphine and heroin.

The potency and availability of these substances, despite their high risk of addiction and overdose, have made them popular both as formal medical treatments and as recreational drugs. Due to their sedative effects on the part of the brain which regulates breathing, the respiratory center of the medulla oblongata, opioids in high doses present the potential for respiratory depression, and may cause respiratory failure and death.

Fentanyl 101

The Facts and Dangers

Fen·ta·nyl
[fen-tuh-nil]

Is a synthetic opiate narcotic, a prescription drug used primarily for cancer patients in severe pain

- Heroin - Cocaine -
- Oxycodone -

and other drugs can be cut with Fentanyl

You can't **see it**, **smell it** or **taste it**

50-100x
more toxic than Morphine

CHAPTER ONE: It's a Trap!

If Lawrence Ponts, known by the streets as Tunes, had known that he would be dead from a fatal neck shot from the .9mm pistol clutched inside the holster on his hip, in the ensuing hour, he would've done things a bit differently. He probably would've made peace with everyone he had wronged over the past decade— the hearts he'd broken, the bar fights he'd engaged in, and settled in his heart that his soul would be transcending to a better place— before he turned on the ignition of his car.

But this was just a normal day. A normal morning. Nothing extraordinary and nothing out of place.

Tunes had many late mornings like this; when the sun shone dully and was a whitish bulb in the midst of the bunch of clouds that filled the sky, filtering lazily only through the holes and pockets it could find in the mist of the daylight sky. The black salon car he rode bumped along the empty 108th street and Kinsman, smoothly like a pregnant beast. He took a sip of the can of beer wrapped in a brown paper bag on his right hand and steered the vehicle with a firm left.

Tunes was never one who would rush things that he could handle. He was someone in the streets; and being in the street required reputation, reputation which he had enough of. He had started out at fourteen by being sneaky. In the latter stages of his career he had learned that all the seduction of sneakiness only got one killed in the line of business he was engaged in. He had a reputation now; and it was that he was vicious. Everyone who knew him called him tunes for a reason. When he played, everyone danced. And Tunes was pleased with his street reputation.

He stole a quick, nervous glance at the baggy jean pants he wore and at his right foot which was deftly pressed on the pedal, his pupils settling on his ankle region. He blinked back momentarily at the road and heaved a sigh of relief.

As long they can't see it, Imma be good.

He looked into the rear mirror, praying for a smirk that never quite cut through the grit of the nervy expression his face wore. He caught the look on the faces of the two passengers who rode with him in the car. Dilla who sat at the back was not particularly concerned about what happened around him. He had the typical disposition of one who was taking a casual ride down the lonely street. He had his cell phone earpiece stuck into both his ears, bobbing his head, and the whispering noise of rap music strained out of the fibers, beating and being heard.

Tunes' eyes tore from him and settled on the other kid riding shotgun with him, and a sense of concern washed over him.

Since Tunes had known Creed, he could swear he never truly understood what the kid was up to, but he had not let that bother him a bit; he could not figure himself out sometimes. It was what kept them all in the business of hustling. Creed, however, was not in the game of hustling; he merely hung out with those who did. People like Tunes. A lean looking kid with sharp features who had been raised in the suburbs, but discovered he had a flair for words and could turn alphabets into words and words into rhythmic sentences of rap music. He had other musical talents that Tunes could attest to but the thrill of living the fast life in slow motion had attracted him like a powerful magnet and himself, a tiny filament of metal, to the top guys in the opioid and heroin drug ring of the inner-city neighborhoods.

"Stupid," Tunes muttered under his breath, so only he heard.

It was Dilla who troubled him. Dilla was doing quite well as one of the network connects of the new opioid drug that was washing through the streets with the mad rushing of overflowing waters. The drug, mud, had earned its name from the actions that followed its use. A Fentanyl based element with a very strong high. It was making millionaires off the streets.

It was Dilla that he had issues with. Creed was just another casualty who got in the way.

Creed mouthed a few words that Tunes could not hear and threw his head afar off to his own side of the car window. Tunes took a swig of the beer he was holding moving the vehicle slowly but surely taking cues from the street signs and turning into each street as if on impulse.

"Making more papers than haters, eh, Lord I pray for the strength to slay fakers, eh."

His words raised up a notch for Tunes to hear, and he couldn't help but smile at the rhyme the kid had just made, stared as he gesticulated with his fingers as though he was cutting through an imaginary head. The action didn't catch him as odd. It was one of the reasons he loved the kid. Creed was ready to lace his bars anywhere and anytime.

Tunes knew that the kid was already cooking his next hit in his head, and it was brewing with rapid effervescence.

When Tunes finally brought the car to a halt in front of a small construction of a house none of both passengers could recognize, an immediate apprehension came upon Creed. The driveway was lined with a thick blackish substance Creed could tell it was oil from a small diesel truck. The engine wrenched with a small cry and stuttered off. Creed stole a look over his shoulder at Dilla and saw that he had also taken down one of the pieces with which he had blocked his ears and was scanning the environment.

"Where the hell is this, brah?" Dilla called out from the back.

All it took was a brief moment for the tension in the car to crash down on them all with all the force of a collapsing stadium. Dilla's phone chimed as it should when a message came in. As he reached into his coat to fetch it, the first movement began quite swiftly.

Tunes unbuckled his seatbelt with the adroit swiftness of a professional athlete and reached for the .9mm that peeked out from where it had been stuck on his right hip. The weapon came up fast and before Creed's mind became alert to what was happening, the narrow hole of the muzzle returned a cold dare to Dilla's face, then his face. His hand flung out instinctively for the gun, slapping it to the right while his body gravitated left and away from the direction of fire. The gun had not fire. He was at once upon Tunes attempting to grab the gun. They fought for an infinite second, each trying to get control of the weapon.

Dilla sat at the back, paralyzed with shock at the private violence that flooded his view in the enclosure.

"The fuck is going on?" He managed to say, after the momentary numbness washed away from his demeanor. What was happening before him was still very strange. Tunes and Creed were engaged in the struggle which held them on a thin line between life and death, and were too occupied to have heard him. Even if they had, none could spare a time to answer the strangest of questions in that situation. Creed, for a man his size, was showing unusual tenacity to dislodge the dangling weapon away from Tunes whose index finger fidgeted around the trigger.

Dilla did what any sensible man in his position would. His hands moved swiftly to unlock the back door of the car, and he stumbled out onto the macadam pavement. What he heard next, stiffened his muscles and brought him to a halt, his stomach flat on the pavement. A gunshot had broken the tussling in the car, the sound reverberating around the street. A group of bird nestled nearby scurried off in fright. An enveloping silence fell on the street afterwards and everything stilled.

He could still hear struggling sounds from inside the car. He turned and saw that a bullet hole was etched on the glass Dilla crawled faster away from the car, his heart pounding hard in its ribcage.

He was a reasonable ten feet away from the car when another gunshot barked. A blood cuddling scream followed. He turned back to see the driver's door opening. What he saw next drained the color from his face.

Tunes appeared as though the upper part of his body had been dipped in a bowl of coagulated maroon paint, staggered out of the driver's seat of the car with both his hands pressed firmly against the right part of his bleeding neck. He swayed for a bit, putting his hand out to grab anything his hand could touch for balance, groping the empty air; he found nothing and his body dropped to the ground like a bag of cement.

Dilla's sagged body picked up with quick adrenaline and he lurched forward to where Tunes' bloody body lay on the fast reddening pool. Tunes was heaving when Dilla's face came over his; searching his eyes for signs of a fight. There was. Tunes' nose raged up and down, trying to pick up as much air as his nose could take, but his body hurled back the oxygen unused. The small pool beside his neck was getting bigger with the passing moments and his eyes blinked with the nude ferocity he had lived with all his life.

When Dilla caught the shivering figure of Creed from the corner of his eyes, the kid was struck numb on his feet. Petrified, he had started to ramble like a mad prophet encountering a possession for the first time. The kid had not intended what had happened; Dilla did not understand what had happened. It had been too fast for his mind to put a lid on.

"Creed," Dilla called out, his eyes never leaving the dying body in front of him. "Listen carefully to what I am about to tell you. Bruh, get the fuck outta here!" Tunes' face had started to become flushed off blood and was assuming the pale blueness of oxygen deprived flesh. "Get the fuck outta here, bruh. Imma handle this."

Creed's mind did not fathom the events that had happened involving him. It was an out of body experience for him, a distinct memory like a dream that faded as soon as the mind was started to comprehend its little details.

Dilla reached for his phone, imputed a few digits into it and put the device to his ear, and waiting for the connection to be rerouted through a secure line. He stood over Tunes' stiff frame, and shook his head. From the corner of his eyes, Creed had begun to jet off in the opposite direction, lurched into a bend and disappeared, gathering particles of dust at his wake.

The sharp beep of the phone notified him that the line had connected. He spoke briefly into it, and listened to what the caller at the end of the line had to say, grunted a few times and the line was severed.

As if on cue, a loud scream pierced through the afternoon heat. He turned to the sound. It was emanating from the small house Tunes' car was parked. Dropping the phone in his back pocket, he took measured steps to the house. He could make out a small hole etched just below the peephole. His eyes darted to the car, to the bullet hole at the passengers' door and traced the trajectory and realization struck home.

The first bullet from the car—which had missed Creed's face by an inch's breath—had pierced through the mahogany door inside. He willed himself to move faster to the house.

It was difficult for him to make out anything from looking through the peephole. He heard the sobbing of a woman, but all his eyes could see was brown paintings on the wall. Opening the door slightly ajar, he saw the little figure of a Caucasian girl laid unmoving in the living room. A pool of crimson had formed a halo around her head. The woman who had been mourning the dead child raised her head up from her kneeling position to catch the shadow that had spied on her grief. Dilla disappeared from the crack. There was nothing he could do now. The child was long dead from the fatal bullet that was shot from the car.

As he raced towards the direction the car had come, he put his mind to action. If the bullet had gone off during the struggle, then it was probably Tunes who had pulled the trigger. The trajectory showed that Tunes must've fired in a bid to knock Creed off. The weapon must've recoiled, and Creed saw the opportunity to even the stakes, by pulling the gun towards himself, gained control and shot him in the neck. An amateur move, but deadly nonetheless.

The sound of police and ambulance sirens echoing faintly in the distance and rushing towards him gave him a better filled mind. He brought his feet to a halt, turned to in the opposite direction and picked his feet faster. It will be difficult explaining himself to the cops. At least, to the cops who didn't know him.

***

By noon, the entire streets had been flooded with ambulance and custom-made police vehicles pulsing blue and red lights, flashing on the houses. A significant portion of the area had been cordoned off by police ribbons, and a makeshift road sign had been erected on the adjoining to wade off traffic coming to the street.

What had been a quiet, tranquil street was now a crowded hubbub of people giving orders and others shuffling about carrying out their orders. The police officers at the scene coordinated themselves like organized orchestra pieces, each part filling into the melody of their discharge of duty. A couple of marked numbers were pegged on the pavement beside evidence scattered on the floor.

Detective Wallace was at the helm of affairs on the crime scene. He had been the first responder on the scene when the precinct got the disturbing news. He stood in between the car and the house, nodding his head and making mental notes. The other police officers knew that disturbing him about their quite insignificant findings would not be a wise thing to do.

When Sergeant Winbush finally arrived some minutes later, he stepped out of the vehicle with his stout body like an animal which had been caged for too long than he had wanted. His big body glided quickly, gravitating towards the black saloon car which had been barricaded by the yellow police caution tape. Inside of the tape was an officer aiming to get a good aspect of the scene for investigation purposes. Winbush gave an irritated sigh when he saw that the house to the left had also been sealed off with tapes.

How had there been two murders on a street that was one of the most serene in the city?

Winbush couldn't place his hand on what his mind struggled to brush off. Two murders, one day… And it was not past noon yet. It undoubtedly was one hell of a day.

Winbush stooped beneath the yellow ribbon and entered into the scene facing the blanketed corpse of one of the victims. The white covering was stained with a thick body of blood on the part Winbush made out to be the head. Winbush cleared the fogginess of his mind at the sight of Wallace who was now issuing notes to an assistant.

"Wallace," He called out to the detective, closing the gap between them. A knowing half smirk appeared on the detective as he turned to his boss.

He faced the police assistant. "Chloe, take a breather and see if you can get any relevant preliminary reports from the forensics team. Don't let me find you."

The attendant nodded and got moving.

"This is a big ass mess, Sergeant. You don't want to know how many people in the neighborhood had taken pictures and videos of what went down," Wallace said, making a beeline for Winbush.

"Shit," Winbush cussed, stealing glances at the windows of the buildings lined up on the street. His eyes roamed and rested on an alcove that the windows had been remained open. As if on cue, a hand reached out slid it shut. Moments later, a white drape fell on the window. Winbush sighed.

"Have the press been here?"

"Not yet." Wallace asserted. Knowing how the press operated in these parts, monitoring Instagram and Twitter accounts of the citizens of Cleveland, Ohio, and it wouldn't take long for them to see a video of the crime scene, and come rushing down with their vans to get juicy firsthand accounts.

"Anybody from the tech department here?"

"Negative, boss," Wallace said. He searched Winbush's face and a thought registered. "What are you planning, boss?"

"Nothing that would get me promoted at the end of the year."

"There's no point to call in the tech crew and turn on the EMP blast. The whole world knows about this now."

"Figures," Winbush grunted and turned to face the corpse on the pavement with a wrinkled frown on his face.

"I don't think he should be any concern to us dead. It's the other one that worries me," Wallace rapped, his voice laced with unease.

A mien of perplexity fell upon Winbush as he scraped his mind in an effort at telepathy. Who is the other person? His features asked as he sustained his looks.

He turned to ask, but Wallace wasn't looking at him now. He was looking at a news van that had screeched to a halt just outside the ribbon. The doors slid open, and a man holding a camera and a tripod jumped out of the van. On his white t-shirt was a bold inscription of KNTV 49, one of the major news outlets of the city in recent times. In seconds, he had leveled the camera on the tripod. A blonde-haired lady dressed in a thick black skirt and white shirt stumbled out after him. She was holding a mic.

She straightened herself, brushed the hair from her face aside exposing the small com device that sat in her left ear. She stood dangerously close to the ribbon and faced the camera.

The cameraman signaled at her with his raised hands and began to close them down one after the other. When all that remained was a tight fist, his lips part to mutter go to the lady.

"Hello, everyone," She spoke animatedly into the camera, his voice, controlled, was filled with years of experience. "My name is Jennifer Corbis, and this is breaking news from KNTV." She paused, like all seasoned newscasters do, and let the effect of those words hit the audience.

"What you're watching behind me is a crime scene the Cleveland Police Department had cordoned off, in the wake of a gun battle that happened moments ago. We have been reliably informed that the incident is drug related, and there were two casualties."

"Reliably informed, my ass," Winbush grunted from where he stood. Whatever happened to good and proper news reporting? Whatever happened to tact?

"We will try to speak with the police to indulge us and throw more light into the issue. Stay tuned."

"Like hell, we will," Winbush smirked. He faced Wallace. "Hope my instructions are still being followed to the latter."

"Yes, boss."

"Now who was the other person John Doe who died?"

"A Jane Doe, sir." Wallace corrected, his voice a tad shaky.

"Who she?"

Wallace opened his mouth to speak, but his voice was drowned when a black luxury SUV screeched to a forced halt, throwing itself forward like a predator that had lost his bearing from over speeding and only checking itself in time.

The news reporter who was trying to get a junior homicide officer to divulge information to her, after seeing the SUV and the men in black matching suits stumbling out—weapons clutched firmly in their grasps, left him feeling like he just stood up at a date, and rushed to the vehicle.

"Oh, my God," Her voice reached a fevered pitch. "In an unprecedented turn of events, the Mayor of Seven Hills, Roberto Ricci has just arrived at the crime scene."

"This is not happening," Winbush when the answer to the question he had wanted to ask seconds ago appeared before him.

A man, wearing a pale blue suit, matching pants, a white shirt and a maroon-colored tie stepped out the vehicle. He was middle-aged from his physical features, although a couple of hairs appeared on the fringes of his head. His had a thick sunglass sitting on most of his face. His lips were pursed. Hard.

He walked steadily to the barrier, walked over it and made a beeline for the sergeant and detectives huddled in a corner. The cops standing on the way made a clear path for him to make his gait smooth.

"Mr. Mayor," Winbush made a move to offer a perfunctory greeting when Roberto checked him with pointed fingers and a brutal glare in his glistening eyes.

"Save it," Roberto said, his voice harsh but shaky. "Where is my daughter?"

"Mr. Ricci if I could explain, the coroner is in there carrying on an investigation report. I offer my condolences to you and the family.

Now, if you would be calm, I can offer to take you in there myself," Winbush managed the most he could offer as a reply, motioning towards the house that was the scene of the murder.

The saying was true; never in the history of being calm had anyone ever been calm because they were told to be calm.

Roberto's laughter contrasted against his shivering frame, giving him a maniacal look. It broke at first like thin glass then it stopped as abruptly as it had started.

"Calm? You want me to be calm? My daughter lies in there, never to rise again, and you ask me to be calm? Would you be calm if it were your daughter?"

It was too important for Jennifer Corbis to ignore. She shivered a cold down her spine and tapped the cameraman. Seconds later, they were live on air again.

"It has been confirmed that one of the Mayor's daughters was one of the casualties of today's fiasco. It is uncertain which of them has died, but we will give you an update as soon as we get them. My name is Jennifer Corbis and this is KNTV News. Stay tuned." She signaled the cameraman to sever the transmission. She leaned her upper body over the ribbon, straining to hear the exchange between the Mayor and the police heads.

"Mr. Mayor, we have in our custody a young lady who had been in the room at the time we arrived," Wallace said, and Roberto's face lit up. Winbush hoped it was not the way he reacted when he had picked someone to pay for his daughter's death. The role of the young lady in the incident had not yet been determined.

Wallace caught his breath and continued. "Our investigators say the apartment was a trap house for black market drugs and the lady and your daughter had been here with the lady for the purchase of this new form of Fentanyl based Heroin called mud."

Winbush watched Roberto's eyes twitch and his body slacken when he heard what he had just said. Smart move, Detective. It was a necessary tactic; throw up a little dirty doing in the face of the aggressive person and they would slow down as if they had been bathed in cold water.

Roberto's eyes shifted to the apartment where a gurney was being wheeled out, the body of his daughter draped in white on top of it. He stormed away from Wallace and Winbush towards the stretcher, and flung the sunglass from his eyes. The coroner assistant who was wheeling the corpse out of the house, scurried off in fright when he saw Roberto approaching with his band of security operatives.

Roberto's blue eyes became watery as he removed the cloth covering her body and saw her still distant eyes staring back at him. For a man who had never been seen crying in public in all his tenure as Councilman and as Mayor, he was managing himself pretty well. Lodged near her wrist was a small brown teddy bear he'd got for her 9th birthday only 3 weeks ago.

When Jennifer saw who was wheeled out, her face went pale in horror, and her body stiffened in shock. She staggered to the ground, but a firm hand grabbed her just before she hit the ground. She stared into the face of the cameraman and muttered a thanks to him.

"We have to start filming now," He said, his voice agitated.

"She's just a kid." Jennifer managed to say.

"We have to start filming now," He said again. Jennifer straightened herself and blinked back the tears threatening to burst out her eyelids and ruin her makeup.

"It has been confirmed," She said, her voice barely audible in the live broadcast. "That the Mayor's 9-year-old daughter, Stella Ricci, was shot in the process of the gunfire. As you can see behind me, the Mayor is standing beside her. Today, Ohio mourns."

Robert grabbed the lifeless body of his daughter and his grief was almost palpable, it smelt like unrestrained rage. He swallowed air in fits of breath and whimpered taking his misery like a lonely child. He stood up with a jerk.

"The bastards who did this would have it coming," he swore, grabbing the teddy bear and closing her eyelids. "They'll pay."

Sergeant Winbush stared at the Mayor as he stood hunched over the little girl, and he suppressed a shiver down his spine. This was going to be a very busy case for the police department. Heck, he knew that Washington would be involved in the entire fiasco, and they will deploy more federal agents to the state. This was not what he had hoped for when he got out of bed this morning. Wallace tapped him on his back, snapping him from his reverie.

"The men recovered forty pounds of mud and a backpack containing clothes in the trunk of the vehicle, and also about a hundred thousand dollars in cash when the house was breached into."

"Jeez." Winbush said.

"That's just the tip of the iceberg, boss. A couple of heavy duty computers was found in the living room. After an intense sweep of the house, about a hundred pounds of mud was found in the ceiling of the house."

Winbush stared wide-eyed at the detective.

"The guy shot dead beside the car was our CI. His name was

Lawrence Ponts a.k.a. Tunes."

Winbush nodded for him to continue.

"The female who was with Roberto's daughter had mud in her pockets. We ran an ID on her. She is Samantha Smith and she claims that Roberto's oldest daughter, Aurora asked her to watch her sister while she picked up a shift at work. Samantha decided then to take the girl with her to score some mud."

"Does Roberto's oldest daughter use mud?" Winbush interrupted with a straight face which was fixed in consideration of the facts that were poured before him.

"It would seem so. Also, our CI was involved with her as a friend. The thing is that Ponts was arrested a few months ago with over a thousand pounds of mud in a box truck. Smart fella hid the mud in bags of chili peppers. Our K-9s were smarter. They picked up the scent and we took him in, remember?"

"Did he sing?" Winbush said.

"He was a tough nut to crack, that one. He did sing after we told him he could face the gas chamber or do life at the federal pen. That was enough motivation he needed. We broke a deal after that. He was to deliver us the top man of the mud ring whom he told us was known only as King and the leader of his gang operation whom he called Mike and then he would be placed on witness protection after that. We kept to our part of the deal and tailed his movements, and obviously, he was keeping to his part when he was unfortunately hit."

Winbush sighed as his brain registered the information. He let his eyes linger on Ricci who was now barking into his phone.

"Any idea on who may have shot him and the girl?"

"Forensics is working on that now. The murder weapon has been bagged and on the way to the lab to check for fingerprints."

Ricci, satisfied that the person at the end of the line got his message, started towards the SUV, his horde of bodyguards circling him and clearing his path. He stopped on his tracks, swung his feet to the left and glided towards the police heads.

"Mr. Mayor," Winbush started, but Ricci silenced him with his raised hand. He closed the distance between them and leveled gaze with him.

"I've spoken with my brother and he will be demanding an inquiry this afternoon. Best be prepared if you don't want to be the next janitor at Adams." And with that, he stormed off and into the back seat of the SUV. The vehicle grumbled, jerked in reverse, and zoomed off from where it had come.

"Shit," Wallace and Winbush said in unison. The Mayor's brother was Antonio Ricci, the Governor of the state of Ohio. They could clearly see the predicament they were in.

"We got to wrap this investigation up urgently, boss," Wallace said, his voice sounding strange to his own ears. "With the Ricci's involved now, this is going to be one giant ass wrecking ball."

"You're right,"

"Boss, I think it's high time we initiate Ghost Protocol. I have a feeling that there may be forces at work here."

"Sounds like a nice plan," Winbush remarked. "I was beginning to think of that."

Winbush raised his hand in the air, and circled his index finger a couple of times, signaling the crew to get things moving. As he made towards his car, his phone vibrated in his pocket. He fished for the device and hit the answer the button.

"Winbush speaking." His voice was firm. He wanted it to be over with. "Who's this?"

"You really should learn phone etiquettes when speaking to a person whose number isn't saved on your phonebook." A knowing grimace struck on Winbush's face as the voice registered in his head. It was a voice he didn't want to hear at the moment. "This is Councilwoman Sara Jackson."

"Ma'am, I—"

"It's all over the news. An assistant just played a clip from KNTV News YouTube page. This mud case is all over the news. Do you know what this means?"

Winbush did, but he felt she knew that already. Three other news vans had pulled up close to the scene and had started filming as the men offloaded packages of mud into their vehicle.

"These incidents are getting out of hand. With the city hall elections coming up in a few months, I will not have you screw this up for me. It's a fucking fiasco right under my nose; drug dealing and shootings? I want you available tomorrow. I'll be flying back in from the capital. Do whatever you can to keep those fucking druggies off my turf," The lady vented and the line went dead before Winbush replied with an affirmative.

Can the day get any worse?

He shoved the first reporter off his path with a light push as when the first reporter approached him for comments on the incident. He did not have the composure to answer their questions just now. He simply made a move for his car, ignoring the throng of reporters who were pushing their microphones into his face.

With a resigned sigh, Winbush got into his car. His cup of coffee he'd brought with him had gone cold he grabbed it. He flung it out the window, started the car and jetted off, heading to the precinct at the other end of the town.

Ghost protocol was their last card to play.

**

Thud after thud, Creed ran. As his feet pounded on the hard earth, the image of Tunes clutching and clawing for air flashed through his mind. The scene played in an iterate fashion.

Nigga pulled a gun on me!

He broke his sprint as he approached a bend, and picked up momentum as his limbs pushed his farther to the one place he had always felt truly safe.

Alyssa's.

He vaulted over the hedge and ranged the doorbell repeatedly in quick intervals. A small crack was all it took. He slid into the building, and with a force he never knew he possessed, he banged the door shut.

His girlfriend, Alyssa blinked in surprise as she accessed the situation: she could barely recognize her boyfriend drenched in blood for most parts of his upper body. He was still breathing fast and hard when he sauntered into the bathroom, the blood clung to his body, stickily, like a needy child clinging to his skin. He turned the faucet and the water gushed out.

"What is going on Creed?" Alyssa cried, standing in yawning mouth of the bathroom's entrance. Creed continued with his activity, his mind distant from the sound and only saw her when she swung into his viewpoint. Still, he couldn't bring himself to divulge anything to her. Not yet.

"Whose blood is this, Creed?" she started into the bathroom and towards him. "Talk to me!"

The reddish liquid sluiced off his flesh and dribbled into the sinkhole of the washing bowl and Creed caught only faint whispers of her talking. He stared into the mirror atop the washing basin, disbelieving the fact that he had just shot Tunes in the neck.

Alyssa's voice was a whimper. She snuggled beneath his body and placed her hand on his chest. The hands nimbly reached down and took the shirt off him. She walked back a distance and threw the shirt a bucket containing her laundry. She walked back and pulled him into a warm embrace, letting the water sluice down her shirt and jean pants.

"Whatever it is, Creed," her voice was now a serenading coo, "It will be alright, I assure you. Just tell me what happened as soon as you can, OK?"

Creed could feel his muscle relax, as he pulled her closer still. His heartbeat slowed down as he leaned towards her and breathed into her moss black hair. She was the only person who could fully understand him, and he could get lost in the moment forever.

The moment was ruined when his phone rung and vibrated in his pocket. Alyssa disengaged from him and grabbed the phone. "Do you want me to pick it for you? Draper's calling."

She took Creed silence as an affirmative. He could've said no, but he didn't. She hit the answer button and placed the phone on speaker.

"Yo, Creed!" The man at the other end hollered, the voice laced with trepidation. "I've been texting and calling you and Dilla all day, man," Draper's familiar voice cut through the fibers of the loudspeaker.

"I swear, Draper, it was an accident. Tunes pulled the gun first and tried to shoot at me. Fuck! He tried to kill me, Draper."

There was a brief thinking silence from the other end of the line and Alyssa could tell that if a pin dropped in the room, it would jolt her from the transfixion her mind was in now. Creed had killed someone.

"Where's Dilla?" Draper asked calmly.

"Dunno," Creed answered, racking his head. "He must've left the scene before the police showed up."

"Listen to what I'm about to tell you."

Creed and Alyssa did.

They didn't like what they heard.

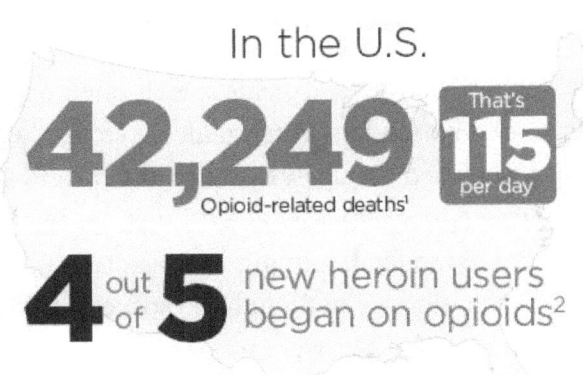

Chapter 2: Fire.

3 Months Ago.

"Ladies and gentlemen," The DJ's voice boomed through the large speakers in the club. "We have come to the highlight of this night."

The noise from the crowd was deafening. The overhead lights blinked, throwing a plethora of vibrant colors down on their faces.

Over the bar section, before a large glass wall lined with a treasure trove of drinks, two bartenders, black males, average height, in their late twenties busied themselves taking orders and serving drinks. They worked mechanically and efficiently, like farmers who knew the lay of the land, moving with a spring in their steps, never brushing each other even though the space provided for striding was not enough. They were wearing blue matching outfits, with a fanny pack strapped on their waists.

The manager of the club always loved it whenever it was time for their shifts: they made enough money and doubled sales targets.

"Y'all put your hands together, as I bring on stage a man who isn't shy to grab the mic…" The DJ paused, scratching erratically on the turntable before him. An alarm effect sounded off. This seemed to get the crowd scattered across the dance floor fired up as they screamed some more. The two bartenders exchanged a knowing smile as their eyes met.

"Give it up for Creeeeeeeeeeeeeeeeed!!!"

A series of fireworks erupted from the stage as the everyone on the dance floor was in high spirits. When the effects died out, a smokescreen filled the stage. In the pitch whiteness of the mist, a figure appeared. He stood still, slouched and staring at the floor. He was wearing a blue sweater with a graffiti colored crown imprinted on it, a white jean pants covering his lean frame and Nike boots.

His head shot up as he brought the microphone that was in his front pocket and grasp closer to his lips.

"Imma be posing as a villain but I fight like a hero

I care about that money, steady stacking up the zeros

I do this for the culture, so best be amazed

Cuz very soon Imma be rapping at the VMAs.

DJ, drop that shit!"

The DJ's hand scratched maniacally on the turntable, and an up-tempo tune wafted through the speakers. The jam was a crowd favorite and seemed to get the people jumping about the place as Creed rapped.

The two bartenders stationed at the other side smiled, as they went about taking orders. One of them stole a glance at the club manager who was seated at the glass cubicle high above where the DJ was standing, was now focused on the rap artist on the stage, nodding his head to the beat. None of the cameras was fixed to them.

It was time to get shit rolling.

When the new set of customers thronged the bar, they unzipped the fanny pack that they wore on their waists, and brought out small wraps of a certain white substance.

Mud, they called it.

It was a substance known to contain doses of Fentanyl mixed with heroin and grounded to powder. It was a dangerous drug known to render the user numb and high. When ingested in high doses, the user could face life-threatening symptoms like paralysis, or worse, death.

As they moved to deliver the drinks, one of them slid the substance discreetly beside the glass.

"Want one?" He said, directing her gaze to the substance.

"Is that—"

"30 bucks." He interrupted her in mid-speech. She fished into her purse and paid for it. She grabbed the wrap, and slid it into her purse. Just before she left, she paid for three more wraps of mud.

And as the rap artist continued to perform on stage, so did the clandestine drug trade linger at the bar section, with the bartenders passing mud to everyone and pocketing the cash.

And as each customer departed the bar, another customer filled the place.

"It's been a pleasure pouring out my heart to you guys. Thank you very much, and do have a wonderful night!" Creed said, after performing for a little over 45 minutes. The crowd cheered him as he dropped the mic on the stage, and walked out through the exit at the back. Creed was a fast-rising sensation in these parts, and he was slowing gathering momentum, with the local TV and radio stations inviting him for interviews and live freestyle shows.

"Yo, Ty and O," Creed said, walking towards the bartenders. "Fix me my special."

By this time, the huge customers at the bar section had dispersed, leaving a smattering of folks on the area. The Jamaican DJ had been replaced with a dude who was playing a mid-tempo song with reduced volume.

"My man!" The bartender named Ty walked to Creed and they did a special handshake: it was a series of fists bumping into each other and ending it all with a dab.

"You killed it tonight. I could feel the energy from here, bruh," The other bartender, O said, as he walked over with two glasses of cold beer. "Drink's on the fucking house."

Creed accepted the drinks with thanks, and guzzled it. He sighed.

"I could get used to this," He said.

Ty's gaze settled on two customers that had appeared at the bar. A Caucasian male in his late thirties, wearing a white checkered shirt with black pants. The brunette lady beside him was donning a blue pleated gown. The makeup she wore was undone, and the freckles on her face was evident. From the way they looked, and the seeming body chemistry between them, Ty could tell that they were together, perhaps married with 2 kids.

"What would you like to drink?" Ty asked. He could tell that the lady was checking him out, with her eyes moving from his face to the well chiseled muscles on his chest region.

The man leaned over and signaled Ty closer.

"We'd like some mud, please." He whispered in a hurry.

One thing that Ty had learned throughout his time dealing drugs to people, is that he worked with his instincts. Every time. And right now, his mind was firing up, sending warnings to his brain.

"I'm sorry," Ty replied, a bit loudly, making sure that his friends O and Creed heard him. "We only have beers, sodas and vodka at the moment."

"C'mon," The man said, his voice low. "We've got good cash here."

O disengaged from Creed and waltzed over to where Ty was. "Yo, man, what's popping?"

"I feel a type of way selling mud to these folks," Ty whispered in O's ear.

"You always feel a type of way selling mud to 'em white breads." O taunted. "I'm fresh out of mud, and I know you got em' with you, so sell 'em nigga."

"How much do you need?" Ty said, facing the man.

"500 bucks." He replied in a casual way. He pointed to his pants, his finger circling the region where his groin was. "I need to get it up. You know how it is." The man's attempt at speaking slangs didn't seem to impress Ty.

Ty unzipped the fanny pack and counted the remaining wraps. It totaled $450. He could make $50 easy from it. In a manner of seconds, money exchanged hands, and the couple was on their way out.

"It's gonna get freaky tonight," Ty heard the man say to his wife as they approached stepped outside. "Let's hurry up. We don't wanna keep Susan waiting in the truck."

White breads, Ty thought and shook his head.

The metallic clock of the bar struck midnight when the trio of Ty, Creed and O, stepped into the parking lot of the clubhouse, entered a grey Chevrolet and zoomed off into the enveloping darkness.

**

6 hours and over 20 miles later on Harvard Road, the noise from the column of cars rent the air in alarming shrieks.

The drivers in their respective cars perspired in the burning heat of the late morning sun, cursing at the cause of the jam.

A certain green truck had ground to a halt near the traffic junction. The controlling light had turned green a little over thirty seconds and any sane driver in that position should have moved the car. But the truck had remained still, the engine whirring idly, as it emitted small puffs of smoke out the exhaust pipe.

The driver riding in a Honda directly behind the truck was furious. The steering wheel creaked under the weight his tight palms curled into a tight fist.

"You've got to be kidding me!" He honked for the umpteenth time. He had a client waiting for him at the office and time was of the essence. He was running late. There was no way he was going to reach the office on time without being ticketed by the cops for over speeding. He gave the pedal a small burst, so his car rammed the backseat of the truck. The truck jerked a few inches and remained static.

He's gonna hear it from me!

The driver unlocked the door and stepped out of the car. Up ahead, the traffic signal was still beeping the green color. He did a mental calculation. In 30 seconds or less, the lights will change to red and I'll be stuck again here with this psycho with a driver's license.

"What the hell are you doing, psycho?!" he exploded as he peered into the driver's compartment. He struck the car with a heavy clenched fist and the metal of the door echoed the energy that it received.

The driver of the car was unmoving and the man's irritation dissipated when the realization struck him.

The truck driver had lost consciousness, passed out; his still eyes staring at nothing in particular on the ceiling of his vehicle with his mouth flying open, ooze dripping out, staining his white checkered shirt and blue pants.

The hell is going on?

His eyes shifted to the passenger's seat to see a brunette lady dressed in a fanciful pleated gown, in a similar position: eyes hollow and distant, body staunch and stiff like a log of timber.

It was when he saw the needle poking out from his right arm, just underneath his elbows, that his fears registered.

They have overdosed on a drug.

"Shit," He cursed. He fished for his phone and dialed 911.

"911, what's your emergency?" A bright voice answered him.

"Harvard Road. Traffic Junction. A couple just overdosed on some drugs." He said and got into his car. He fired it up and swerve the car to the side and skidded past the truck. As he floored the pedal, he thought he saw a young girl plopped at the back of the car.

He brushed the thought aside as he took a bend and gunned the car forward. There was no way any cop will give him a ticket when an emergency was in the works.

Detective Wallace Friggs of the Cleveland Police Department sat in his small rectangular office plopped at the end of the precinct hall. His eyes were fixed on his phone while he adjusted his white-collar shirt. He looked cool, calm and collected as he flipped through his Facebook news feed.

A man in his mid-forties, Wallace had the look of a man who had seen the great ills of the world, and had decided to fight them one day at a time.

Behind him, a plethora of medals, trophies and plaques splayed the wall, a recognition of the many years of intuitive police work, brilliant detective and tactical acumen. He was a well-respected man of the Police Department in Cleveland.

He had been tipped to become the Captain of Police, but political bureaucracy and a lot of paperwork seemed to hinder the process. It didn't bother him one bit. He just wanted to do his job and go back home to meet his lovely wife and two kids and sleep on his bed, satisfied that the streets were free from the bad guys. That was all that mattered to him.

Three knocks on his door, jolted his gaze from his phone. His stared at the intruder standing at the entrance of his office.

It was his police assistant, Chloe. She was the best graduating student of her set in the Police Academy and when she was posted to the division, he took her under his wing.

"What's the matter, Chloe?"

"We just received an emergency," She said, approaching his desk. "The caller called in an incident on Havard Road. A couple had overdosed on some drugs. And ambulance and traffic wardens within the area have been alerted and are already on their way there."

He was already up before she finished what she had to say. He grabbed his holster on the table and strapped it on his hip. She followed him out of the office, out the busied hall, and into the precinct's parking lot.

Wallace moved with a spring in his steps. He located his navy-blue Toyota Corolla between two custom made police vehicles. He got in, and Chloe settled beside him.

The car hissed and slid out of the parking lot into the blazing morning heat.

Chloe watched her boss as he meandered and sped through traffic, his eyes fixed on the road, his fingers firm on the wheels. She couldn't have been happier to have been selected by Wallace himself to work under his unit. The professionalism he put into the cop work quite intrigued her. She'd learn a few things every time she went on the field with him.

He swung the car to a halt within an inch's breath from the ambulance. For some reason, he reached into the pigeonhole and retracted a sunglass. Putting it on, he got out of the car.

Chloe followed closely behind, as the traffic wardens directed other motorists to use the other lane.

Wallace stared at the couple in the car, and stared in surprise at the oddity. He wasn't new to this type of scenario before, but he'd never seen a couple rendered unconscious as a result of an overdose at this time of the morning.

He dipped his hand into his pocket to fish out his gloves. Ruining a scene was the last thing he wanted to do. He unlocked the driver's door, held his breath and retracted a small plastic bag containing a white substance that was resting on the floor. As he strengthened himself, a little movement flew into his line of sight. From the backseat.

What he saw next drained the color from his face. Immediately, he raised two fingers in the air signaling the team of paramedics over.

There's a kid in the backseat!

He signaled the paramedics over.

The officers dashed towards the vehicle, wearing face masks and Narcan spray held firmly in both their hands. A paramedic grabbed the kid from the backseat. Too weak to struggle against this foreign control of her body, the kid obliged the hands that probed his body for evaluation and treatment. She did not speak, and the occasion continued in a heavy silence.

Wallace tried to make sense of the plastic bag that had been found on the scene. He held it up for the umpteenth time and observed the printing it bore; an amber flame burning with a motionless flicker. Nothing different was added when he scrutinized it over again. He shoved it into the evidence bag he carried along with the syringe which had been found on the deceased man's person.

"Chloe, when we get back to the precinct, get these items to forensics," Wallace said, handing the evidence bag to her. "I have a feeling that this is a new substance, and we need to act fast. Start evacuation protocols. The traffic is something else."

**

If anyone in the neighborhood where Mike lived knew what he was doing behind closed doors and drawn curtains, they were too afraid to speak to the cops. Even the neighbors with least racist sentiments could sniff out the fact that he was doing something illegal and that was what attracted many people to his house all time of the day. The junkies knew for certain that he was a drug pusher and a peddler.

With an unsteady composition of violence, anger issues and a general distrust of society with the exception of his small circle, Mike seemed to be the quintessential drug dealer of the city. At the tender age of twelve, he started dealing illegal drugs to the school he attended. It was the only way he could provide medications for his ailing single mother who had been stricken with cancer. When the cops carried out raids in the school, he would carefully conceal the bag containing the contraband in the chemistry lab. He'd found out earlier on that police K-9s found it difficult to pick off the scent of the various contraband he peddled—weed, codeine, cocaine and free base—when their sense of smell is crinkled up as other similar smell wafted and jumbled up their decisiveness. This he did, till his mother died.

He dropped out of school shortly and focused on pushing weed, cocaine, crack and heroin on the streets, the clubs, the movie theaters, the sports arena and anywhere he knew people would need it.

Two decades later, he had steadily built a reputation for himself in the streets.

Money. Power. Respect. Loyalty. These things were important as the breaths that coursed through his lungs. He would never let anything jeopardize that process. His own band of drug peddlers—

Ty, O, Draper, Tunes, Mileana, Neicesa, Dilla, and Tat knew that, and it was why they sat and stood huddled at the backyard of his house—smoking and drinking beer from red plastic cups—and watched as he busied himself, slamming his fist into a dark-skinned man too bloated to defend himself. The ambiance of the backyard was misty-like, the smokes from their cigarettes floating around the air like butterflies.

"No one steals from me!" Another fist smashed into the man's face, punctuating Mike's words. The punch seemed to pummel him to the floor, and when the band who watched the fiasco thought the onslaught would dissipate, Mike turned his legs to a wrecking ball, kicking him repeatedly as crimson flew out of his mouth in short bursts.

The man was hovering in the chasm between consciousness and unconsciousness when out of the corner, Creed appeared, bearing a bag containing burgers.

"Yo, Mike!" He dropped the package and rushed to where Mike was and tried to get between them. "Yo man, chill man, bro!"

Mike ran the options of taking Creed out of the way with his bloodied fist and thought better of it; Creed wasn't exactly a member of his band, and the rules didn't apply to him.

"Creed, get out the way man," He said testily, his gaze leveled with the intruder.

"Nah, bruh. You gon' knock his lights out. I won't stand here and watch you kill a black man."

"A black man that steals from me? Bruh, this bitch ass nigga dropped by the house and told me he wanted to get some fire. He ain't got no cash on him, so I showed his ass the door."

Fire was another contraband that Mike pushed on the street. It was the new high every junkie on the streets needed, if they could afford it. The Fentanyl percentage in this drug was twice higher than in mud, and so implications of ingesting it was enormous. Fire was a tad expensive to purchase and to push, and Mike was always ready for every circumstance. He opted to peddle it at exotic bars where he knew the bigwigs of the city who needed to get a little fun would flock.

Mike tried to bypass the man standing between him and his nemesis, but Creed was faster. Heaving a defeated sigh, he continued. "After we left the house for our rounds, our cameras picked him up breaking into the house and into the stash room. Bitch stole 5 grams of my fire! He has to pay, nigga."

"Mike, look at him! Take a good look at him, man. He sure don' paid the price. Just chill out."

Mike lifted his gaze over his shoulder and rested it on the dark-skinned fella. He had beaten him to a pulp; he saw the man had curled himself into a ball and he shook his head.

"Ty, O," He called out, turning to face the band. "Take this bitch outta here. Drop his ass at the stop sign and leave his monkey ass there!"

Creed did a mental calculation. The nearest hospital to the stop sign was six blocks away. The fiend had a chance of survival if someone would take him to the hospital on time. Knowing that that area was a busy street, it would be easy getting help.

Ty and O swaggered to where the man was curled up, lifted him up like he weighed nothing and walked out of the backyard. Moments later, the noise of a car jetting off filled their ears.

Mileana stopped up and rushed into the building. When she came back, she was holding a small bowl containing water in one hand, while a dry napkin rested on her shoulder.

"Thank you," Mike said, as she leaned over to wash his bloodied fists. His eyes were transfixed on her mounds of flesh, and he wondered for a brief moment if any man would ever say no to explore the curvy creature that was before him. He brushed the thought aside as quickly as it had come. This wasn't a time to get freaky.

Ty and O returned shortly from their trip and joined the others at the backyard of the house. They ebbed closer to Mike. Creed grabbed his bag of burgers on the ground and passed it around to all of them, and they started munching, while small chatter filtered amongst them.

"Aye, Creed," Neicesa said, her voice calm and soft. "Can you do a freestyle using all our names?"

"Is that a dare?" Creed smiled at her.

"If you say so." Her eyes dared him. Ty and O already used to this kind of scenario started beat boxing with their mouth. Creed steadied himself, nod to the beat a few times, and began to rap.

"Every time I step into the court y'all know I be ballin' like Mike

Hear my people scream whenever little Creedo grabs the mic

I'm making money moves till I can get a Rose to Diana

But yo Mileana, can we do something nasty in a cabana?"

"OOOOOOOOOOO" Everyone except Mileana screamed.

"Apologies to that, baby, but you fine like Neicesa

But I can't hit that when she be looking like my sister."

Neicesa flung the plastic cup she held at him, but he ducked just in time as both cup and contents flew past his head. Everyone burst out laughing. Creed continued like nothing happened.

"Haters can hate, but I ain't got no time for that

All I wanna do is grab a tit...for Tat

Cuz I'm a shot caller, call me Ray Dilla

I'm a God on the mic, ain't nobody realer

Very soon, my face gon' be on the headline news

Making y'all rap and dance to my Tunes

Shoutout to my niggas Draper, Ty and O

I'm that dynamite, get ready for me to blow.

Man, I'm out."

"Man, you killed it," Mike said, his voice animated. This was the reason why he kept Creed around. Creed was the one who changed his mood. Creed moved around throwing handshakes with the men, and mouthed a little to the ladies who hugged him anyway.

"Creed, you need mud or fire? Name it, I'll give you a couple of bags."

"Mike, you know I don't roll like that," Creed replied, smiling and shaking his head. "Besides, what's the first rule of drug dealers?"

"Never get high on your supply," Everyone chorused in unison. It was a strict rule Mike made them follow. Anyone who got caught ingesting mud or fire will face grave consequences from him. Turning to face the band, Mike said. "How much did y'all make from last night?"

Ty spoke first. "We cleared all our muds, Mike," He gestured towards O. "10 bands neat."

"Us, too" Meleana said, smiling. She worked shifts with Neicesa as exotic dancers at the other end of the town, selling fire and mud to VIPs who stalked the place and requested their services on private booths.

"It was a drag at first, but I managed myself pretty well." Tunes said. He stalked cinemas and theatres and sold his portion of his drugs in-between movies and shows.

"I almost got shot by the police last night," The one called Tat who stationed at all the laundromats said. "I cleared everything when I got into the other street,"

"I cleared mine too," Dilla said, smiling weakly. Dilla was not a man who talked much. Beside him, Draper smiled. He never went on runs like the others. His job was to keep the money and the drugs safe and discover hot spots in the city for the drug trade. Mike ran the numbers in his head and smiled. 60 bands in one night! Business was good.

His phone vibrated in his pocket. When he saw the caller, he excused himself and took a slow stride to the front of the house. A car careened from the far end of the street into theirs and pushed itself to the front of Mike's house just as he was stepping on the curb. A couple of drunk college boys were in the car. Mike looked down both ends of the street and gave them the signal to come towards him. The guy riding shotgun stepped out and swaggered towards Mike.

He discreetly passed a roll of notes into Mike's hand and Mike whispered into the kid's ear. The kid nodded his understanding and they withdrew from each other, and he ran back to the car. Mike made his way back to the porch as the car made its way towards the end of the driveway near the fire hydrant. They upturned a loose patch of grass and picked out the package with a fire label on it. They moved away faster than they had arrived.

Mike smiled. Drug business was good business.

<u>Chapter Three: Sinful World</u>

The Cleveland Police Department stood a towering fifteen stories high, deep in the heart of the city. Out in front, a smattering of pedestrians walking briskly, and cops chatting lightly, drinking hot coffee wrapped in brown cups. The sun overhead poked out of the clouds like a shy lover, its rays seemed to filter through the bulbous clouds and pierced the treetops, casting shadows on the pavement.

Inside the precinct, activities dragged on with a hum; police filing paperwork for perps for jaywalking, over speeding, and minor crimes. The atmosphere at the police command center had taken a different ambiance.

Located below a flight of stairs, twenty feet under the ground, the command center was designed to keep everyone in, in the event of a terrorist attack or natural disaster.

It was rarely utilized. It was only used in rare cases where recent events proved to be difficult to handle with the usual police work. And the moment called for one. In its walls sat twelve policemen and women around a roundtable that opened up to a wall containing clippings and marked writings, a map of the state and a large LED screen.

The cops seated at the table consisted of forensic agents, the tech crew, traffic wardens and a police assistant. Sitting at the head of the table was Detective Wallace Friggs. He had summoned the crucial meeting at the wake of the recent fiasco that happened a little over 96 hours.

"Chloe," Wallace beamed to his assistant. "You have the floor."

"Thank you, detective." Chloe said, standing up from where she stood. She moved seamlessly, her flat shoes making little noise as she made her way to where the screen was.

"Good morning, everyone,"

"Good morning, Chloe." They all chorused.

She faced the enthusiastic eyes that peered back at her. She steadied herself, took two sharp breaths, and spoke.

"While the fight for crack and heroin persists with a recorded number of arrests, a greater enemy arises," She fiddled with the remote on her hand, and pointed it to the screen. A single word appeared on the screen.

FENTANYL.

"Fentanyl," Chloe repeated, her voice breaking the silence in the room. "For those of us unfamiliar with the subject, Fentanyl is an unbelievable potent synthetic drug that has been tipping the scales since it began to be abused by residents of Ohio. It was formerly used as a painkiller to soothe cancer patients and people going through chronic pains after intensive surgery." The screen showed a doctor administering a few doses to a bedridden patient.

"That was until someone realized how it could be monetized on the black market. Like morphine and other opioids, fentanyl basically works by binding to the opioid receptors in the body, located in areas of the brain that control pain and emotions." An electronic image of a brain appeared on the screen.

"When the fentanyl binds to these receptors, it increases the dopamine levels in the brain's reward centers and produces an intense state of euphoria and relaxation. In reality, Fentanyl doesn't only carry out that function alone, but also attaches itself to the opioid receptors located in other areas of the brain, especially the ones that control breathing." She paused as the screen showed a white substance that began spreading across a digital brain. "While fentanyl creates a long lasting high for people who ingest them, it has grievous consequences."

"What's the difference between fentanyl and heroin?" asked a middle-aged traffic officer from where he sat.

"While both drugs bind to the opioid receptors in the brain, the chemical composition of fentanyl's allows it to arrive at the opioid receptors much faster than heroin. It is also a known fact that Fentanyl also reacts more tightly to the opioid receptors than any other opioids."

"Speak English, please." Another man said. "Say I'm a ten-year-old kid, how would you explain it to me?" The hall vibrated with light chuckles. Detective Wallace wore a vexed expression on his face and stared them all down till the laughter died into silence.

"It means that only a small amount of fentanyl is needed to react to cause harm. As a result, a minuscule dose of fentanyl can have the same lethality as a much larger dose of heroin. I do hope your ten-year-old self can understand that."

The command center erupted with laughter. Chloe waited for the moment to die down, but it was taking forever.

"Now, we already know Fentanyl is bad in the wrong hands, and cocaine and heroin aren't our friendly neighborhood drug. What happens when you combine fentanyl with heroin?"

She hit the remote and the digital brain vanished and was replaced with a morgue shot of a man and woman.

"Ladies and gentleman, showing on the screen is the couple we found dead in a truck. That's Lucas and Gail Vincent. After discovering the stash found within their persons in the car, an intensive coroner's report was carried out. The substance they had overdosed on was a mixture of the two quite deadly compositions, known by the streets as Mud. And he ran the percentage index, and discovered that the fentanyl compound was higher per gram molecule.

"Over the past 4 days, we have surprisingly garnered a number of homicides cases as a result of an overdose on fentanyl-based drugs, and the numbers from the counties are crippling."

She moved forward to point a section of the large map. "In Cuyahoga county alone, there have been 15 deaths reported over the past week due to overdose on this mud and another potent drug call Fire. Fentanyl is being sold under the guise of painkillers such as Oxycodone. In the last 3 days, Seven Hills, East Cleveland, Euclid, Garfield Heights and Maple Heights have recorded cumulative seventy homicidal cases as a result of an overdose. The few ones who have managed to survive are at the Cleveland Clinic and the University Hospitals of Cleveland, and they are having a hard time getting back on their feet. These drugs are known to be addictive and once someone gets hooked on it, it will be impossible to let go."

"And that is why we need to act," Wallace said, standing up and taking the floor. He moved to the section where the clippings were positioned and stood there. The clippings were made to look like a set of pyramids. "We don't know the perps who have flooded our streets with these drugs mud and fire. We do know that it might be a drug-trafficking ring moving large amounts of drugs, and we need to get these drugs off the streets for good."

He faced the room with a stern look on his face. "We need to pin faces to these John Does here. Time is already against us. The homicides are increasing every day. We owe it to ourselves and to our friends and family to be their last line of defense. If you see anything out of the ordinary, dock it in. Questions?"

Half a minute later, he called the meeting to an end and ushered everyone out. As he made his way to the elevator outside, he tapped Chloe.

"I gotta say I loved how you handled yourself at the briefing."

"Thank you, sir" She smiled. "I learn from the best."

"Hey, what about the child from the incident on Harvard Road"

"She's recuperating pretty fast, but she's in no mood to talk."

"Okay. Keep me posted on that as soon as possible."

"Copy that."

***

Chapter Four: Root of All Evil

80th and Detroit

A hooded figure waited out in the alley, his fingers gingerly caressing the illegal firearm aimed and ready to fire. Sam had a score to settle, and he would make sure that he did. He was well hidden from the lights that flooded the walkway of the streets, but the bandage that wrapped most of his body was evident.

He was pretty banged up from the onslaught his frail body received from a thug named Mike who peddle and stashed fire and mud at his house. He had approached Mike and tried to broker a deal with him, for a package of fire. Mike had asked for payment in cash, which he didn't have, but offered his gold wristwatch, instead. Mike told him that he had no use for the thing, and drove him out of the house.

When he came back later that evening with the cash that Mike had requested, there was no one at the residence. It was easy getting into the house, and he had helped himself with the wraps of mud that was splayed on the table. But he had wanted fire and had seen one of Mike's boys, Draper go into the adjacent room and came back shortly with a big package containing fire. He had walked into the stash room and grabbed a large package of fire and stumbled out of the door.

Mike was waiting for him outside, bloodshot eyes and an intent to kill. He had immediately offered the cash he brought, but Mike was having none of it. He had grabbed him against his pleas, tied him up in the basement till the next day, when he brought him out the backyard of the building, took the cash and the gold wristwatch, and made a public show of shame of him.

He had mangled him up and beat him to a pulp. His band of drug dealers watched him as blow after blow smashed into his skin. He had been clinging with faint grasp to his dear life when a young boy had jumped in to intercede, and brought the beatings to an end. He was dumped by the roadside and left for dead.

When he had regained consciousness, he was blinking back at a white bulb glowing at his face. He had thought he was in heaven, when a doctor approached he rested and told him he had been unconscious for the past 3 days. A good Samaritan had brought him to the hospital and had paid for his medications and treatments. The doctor had inquired about his condition and Lucas had lied that he was mugged by a band of robbers. It was a good lie. The doctor believed every word of it. Then she excused herself to tender to a patient who was in the ER.

When the doctor came back, Sam wasn't there anymore. He had slinked out of the room and into the utility compartment, stole a janitor's overalls and limped out of the hospital.

He had one resolve on his mind when he got home and had opened the illegal firearm he'd purchased from a black market dealer. He wanted revenge! And killing Mike would bring him the satisfaction he needed.

The box truck Tunes drove broke the silence of the midday quietness as it swung into the street and ease to a stop just outside the driveway of one of the high-rise buildings. Ty and O jumped out almost immediately and started up the flight of wooden stairs into the house. They had worn large shirts which seemed to conceal the handguns they strapped on their hip pockets. Tunes fiddled with the keys, and got down eventually, and was about to take the stairs when a voice broke out.

"Hey Tunes, I need some of that fire!"

Tunes turned to the sound. A woman was rushing towards him, her nightie flailing in the evening wind.

Sam stood from where he was and cussed, his face held disappointment and resentment.

He had come for Mike, and the fucker didn't follow them. The .9mm he held was still pointed at the last man to get out of the truck. Tunes, he figured the man was.

Well, someone gotta pay. He leveled the weapon with the man's face, the silencer lodged over the barrel.

"Can I get the ground chuck, Tunes?" the voice turned to a plea. Tunes cussed. It was the neighborhood junkie, Debbie. She was always in need of fire, especially when she had no cash to pay for them.

Tunes paid no attention and started up the stairs, but he wasn't prepared for what happened next.

Bang! Bang! Bang!

Three successive shots whizzed out from a gun across the street. Tunes ducked in time as the bullet swam across, barely grazing his forehead. His mind was on overdrive. Throwing caution to the wind, he grabbed the junkie and used her as a shield. Good choice he had made; only a second later a couple of slugs had sunk into the limp frame of the woman. Tunes ran the options he had. If he made the race to the house, he would be a sitting duck. He unstrapped his weapon from his hip, and fired a couple of double taps to the alley. He could hear the bullet hitting a couple of metal bins splaying their contents on the floor.

Tunes wondered if the others inside had heard the fire and were deliberately ignoring him to die in these streets. Anger surged from within him towards no one in particular. Of course, they did; they had heard spitfires from outside the building but they didn't think much about it. Gun fires in the dead of night was a regular thing if you lived in the street. Ty had taken a female companion that had been in the house to a separate room. O busied himself, bundling mud into their packs.

"Motherfuckers!' Tunes cursed and swallowed a huge dose of cold air which quickly ran to his lungs. A bullet whizzed past his ear, and then it died. Tunes figured the shooter was reloading the weapon, and he made a break to the truck with dizzying speed, fired up the engine. The car responded at the first spin of the key and coughed to life. Tunes quickly but the gear in reverse ducking beneath the steering wheel, stealing little glance upwards for direction, he bumped into the street and returned the gear to acceleration. He fired recklessly down the road as the bullets trailed him.

The body of Debbie lay spread-eagled on the pavement, the nightgown she wore billowing in the wind. Crimson trickled from her chest and ran into the pavement.

Sam seeing what he had done, and disappeared back into the alley, limped a couple of blocks into the next street. He fished for his handkerchief and wiped the weapon clean. He looked for the nearest bin his eyes could find, and discarded the weapon there. Soon after, he flagged down a driver, got in and vanished into the night.

***

The smoke fizzled out from the car into the night air and dispersed as quickly as it had formed. The cop inside reclined on the seat and stared vacantly into the quiet road. He was on night patrol to report and ticket over speeding drivers and jaywalkers, and the coffee which he held was the only thing that kept him from grabbing at the blanket at the backseat and falling asleep. All the radio stations at this time of the night were transmitting low tempo blues which only seemed to worsen his current situation. He fiddled with the tuning knob on the car stereo, and happened on a station. The on-air personality was already speaking enthusiastically.

"The drug situation in Cleveland is alarming," the voice said. For some reason, the cop seemed to let his fingers linger on the knob. He increased the volume and relaxed back in the seat.

"The police are having a hard time bringing the drug peddlers pushing drugs fire and mud to book. Till date, I don't think any arrests have been made and this is not the best for Ohioans. We're still trying to find a way out of illegal possession of firearms, and now drugs?! The heck is going on?"

But the officer wasn't listening anymore. His eyes had flown to the speed tag that was stationed on the stereo. The electronic screen was flashing with bright red lights.

75/60!!!

He eyes flew to the road, and what he saw made his hands move instinctively to turn the ignition of the car and swayed the car into the road. A box truck had jetted past, and given the time, it seemed unusual. For one, it was a box truck. Over speeding was not the MO of drivers of the box trucks, and from the way the truck was jetting off, his instincts were on the red. And his instincts were never wrong.

Another drunk driver, he thought, and he switched gears, and grabbed the police siren that was resting on the panel and hung on top of the vehicle. He honked the car a few times, but the truck made no intentions of slowing down, as it picked up momentum and displaced the cop car.

He smiled as his left hand flew into his pocket to grab the coms. He steered the car with a firm right.

The stubborn ones are the best people to chase down. He radioed Police HQ.

"Dispatch, this is Officer Martin Hayes 115354," He spoke matter-of-factly. "In hot pursuit of a white box truck."

"License plates?" The female voice said in a monotone.

"Can't make 'em out," He spoke as he floored the pedal. "Request backup to cut him off at the next junction."

"Roger that." The voice said with finality of tone.

***

Tunes faced a more significant problem as he swung the truck into a sharp left and lurched the truck forward. He had only escaped being murdered on the streets, and now a police was after him?

Fuck! Fuck! Fuck! Fuck! He cursed as he stole a short glance at the rearview mirror. The cop sped dangerously close to the truck and rammed it from the back. The truck screeched and swerved to the left. He grabbed the steering wheel and swung the truck a hard right. The truck grumbled in protest and got into the road.

Fuck!

He floored the pedal again and looked at the mirror. He turned on the sirens; it was throwing blue and red light and the alarm was blaring, piercing the cold night it chased after him. He grabbed his firearm that was resting beside his legs and opened the drop latch between the seats. He decelerated the truck, and when he saw that the cop was gearing up to ram him again, he dropped the weapon and closed the latch and gunned the truck forward.

He had only moved for a couple of seconds when he saw before made him realized that it was the end of the road for him.

A roadblock had been set up ahead and a couple of police cars blinked back at him.

There was nowhere to go.

Fuck!

He swung the truck to a halt outside the parking lot of Loan Max and turned off the engine.

"Get out of the truck and place your hands behind your head." A voice from a megaphone boomed.

Tunes obeyed as any honest civilian would and the officers moved towards him slowly. His head was slammed on the bonnet of the truck as a couple of hands frisked him. Tunes had a lopsided grin on his face as they'd found nothing on him. Discarding his firearm was a smart move. He was handcuffed. A policewoman walked over to him and read him his Miranda rights and marched him to the back of one of the cars locked him inside.

Tunes watched as a couple of policemen marched to the truck and started searching it.

If they kept on with the act, he may be tagged for over speeding and made to pay a fine, and that was it. They had found the usual ice cream supplies and were about calling it a night when a police car glided to a halt close to the truck.

A cop stumbled out and opened the back door. Two German Shephard dogs jumped out and Tunes knew there and then that he was in serious trouble. His face perspired even though the ac vents of the vehicle was whirring idly.

He prayed silently.

The dogs began to sniff every nook and cranny of the truck. Upturning every plastic containing spilling the sour liquid on the floor. One of the dogs was particularly clawing at the plywood walled interior and barking irritably. The policeman who bought the dogs tried to dissuade the dog.

"C'mon boy, let's get outta here."

But the dog kept clawing at the wall. The cop stepped into the van and tapped the wall. He could hear the noise of something spilling over. He signaled the others over and explained the situation to them.

Moments later, the wall came crashing down as a hammer tore through it. A big sack sat inside. They stared at each other and hefted the sack outside. When they opened the bag and found what was staring back at them, their faces wore surprised looks.

It was a bag of chili peppers.

They were still undecided on what to do with the bag when the German shepherd wiggled out of his handler's grasp and knocked the sack over spilling the contents on the ground. Amongst the chili pepper were small wraps of a white substance with a fire emblem and another with 'M' written boldly on it.

They checked inside the bag, and found to their dismay that the small packages filled with more than half of the sack.

Tunes knew that it was no use praying.

It was over for him.

***

Detective Wallace Friggs had already tucked his daughters to bed and kissed his wife good night, and was floating in dreamland when the sharp ringtone of his phone pulled him back to consciousness.

He blinked at the screen and gave a short gasp.

"Wallace speaking," His voice was gruff. "This better be good."

He listened as the voice at the other end filtered to his ears. Moments later, he was fully dressed and out in the driveway of his house. He slid into the car, started the engine and drove out of the driveway.

He was smiling.

It was good alright.

***

Detective Wallace Friggs of the Cleveland Police Department stepped into the precinct with purpose on his steps. Chloe was waiting for him at the foot of his office, a blue file resting on her arm. Wallace wondered if she ever took a break from police duties at all.

"The perp is waiting at the interrogation room, sir," She said, smiling as he handed his dossier. Wallace flipped through the pages, his eyes roving at the details therein.

"Has anyone gone in to question him?"

"No, sir. The officer-in-charge, Martin Hayes says you should do the honors."

"Is Captain Winbush around?"

"Not yet. But he was informed of our briefing last week."

"Good. Good." Wallace said, walking towards the terrace leading to the interrogation room. He found the officer-in-charge, Martin Hayes looking through the plexiglass at the perp inside the interrogation room.

"Well done, Officer Hayes," Wallace said and shook his hands. The officer smiled sheepishly. He disengaged and walked to the corner and opened a drawer. When he came back, he was holding an evidence bag containing a firearm.

He explained everything he knew to Wallace who smiled at the thoughtfulness of the cop. He was happy that the expert police for which he was highly revered was rubbing off these young bucks.

"Well done, Officer." Wallace beamed. He handed the evidence bag to Chloe. "What the temperature of the room?"

"10 degrees Celsius."

"Good enough," Wallace said. It was a psychology thing, Wallace thought. Wallace, from intuitive police work, had devised a method which seemed to get perps talking if they didn't want to.

Leave them freezing out for a couple of minutes, and they would do anything to get out of there.

***

The freezing temperature of the interrogation room made Tunes shiver. His breaths were slow and measured as he sat under the bright glow of the blueish bulb that hung on the ceiling. He rubbed his handcuffed palms together trying to create heat for himself. When the door creaked open, he was thankful for the humid air that wafted into the room. It was short lived as the door was banged shut.

Detective Wallace Friggs walked into the room, sat down at the seat facing the perp, crossed his legs and absentmindedly flip through the pages of the file in his hand. This he did for over 2 minutes. It was also a psychology thing Wallace did to disorient perps who were about to be questioned.

"Quite a resume you got here," Wallace said, lifting his eyes from the dossier. "Real name: Lawrence Ponts, known in the streets of Cleveland by many Aliases. Dagger. Shadow, and most recently, Tunes."

Wallace stood up from the seat and walked around the room. "Dropped out of high school to be remanded in a juvenile prison for illegal possession of cocaine, and you have been radio silent ever since till now."

Tunes shifted in his seat. He wanted to get out of here.

"You were arrested this evening on counts of speeding over the designated limit. You were doing 75 on a 60, and disregarded a direct police order to pull your truck over."

"I want my lawyer." Tunes said.

"But that's not the only reason why you're right here," Wallace said, as though he never heard Tunes' request. "A bag of fentanyl-based drugs—mud and fire they call it on the streets—was found on your truck neatly concealed under a bag of chili peppers. Over 40 pounds of drugs! What can you say for yourself??"

"I want my lawyer." Tunes said.

"From the way I see it, when you leave this room, you'll find yourself in a courtroom, and before you can say mud, you're already on your way to a federal penitentiary where you'll be placed for the rest of your life, that is even if you survive the first 3 months."

"I want my lawyer," Tunes said. He could barely recognize his voice.

"But that wasn't the only event that happened this evening, huh?" Wallace broke his strides and turned to face Tunes. "You were fleeing from a murder scene tonight, weren't you?"

"I want my lawyer."

Wallace smiled at the perp. He was a tough nut to crack. But all nuts do crack in the end. Wallace removed a photo from the dossier and placed it before Tunes.

"Do you know Debbie Walsh?"

Tunes stole a quick look at the photo. It was Debbie alright. Except this time, her eyes were vacant and lost.

"I ain't know no junkie named Debbie Walsh. I want my lawyer."

"Aha! But I never mentioned that she was a junkie."

Realization dawned on Tunes. He had made a big mistake.

"She was one of your customers?" Wallace leveled his face with the criminal. "We found two different bullet shells from the murder scene. One is still being identified. The second belonging to you."

"I want my lawy—"

"During the police chase, you threw away your weapon. The cop car ran over it, and the officer after bringing you in acted on his instincts to go back the route you took. The pavement around 80th and Detroit is smooth with no speed-breakers. He found a firearm matching the bullet shells lying in the middle of the road. He took it to forensics to scan for fingerprints, and it came back with a 100% match. Yours."

"I want—"

"If I'm correct and I'm usually correct, a murder charge and illegal possession of a firearm have just been added to your rap sheet. You will not only go to a federal pen, but you will be placed in solitary confinement."

Tunes' face went pale in horror. There was no way he was going to do time in a federal pen. He heard about things that happened to people who got transferred there. Plus, he was gonna be placed on solitary confinement?

"I know what you're going to say next," Wallace said, taking a slow stride to the horrified Tunes. "Blah blah blah you want your lawyer."

Wallace's face was an inch's breath away from Tunes'

"Your lawyer can't help you."

And with that, Wallace strode out of the interrogation room to meet the amazement on the policemen's faces who had been watching the whole action from the other side.

"Boss, you broke him pretty bad," Chloe said, grabbing the dossier from the detective.

"Now, we wait for the next phase to begin. That guy right there? He will lead us to whoever is running this drug operation in the state. Please tell the technician to increase the temperature in the room. The last thing we want is him dying from the cold before we ever get a chance to wrap this thing up."

***

Keno Getty woke with a start. He strained to see in the dark, and ran his hands over the headboard till he found the light switch. He flicked it on, and as the light flooded his bedroom, he reached for the blasted phone that had woken him up.

"Keno Getty." He yawned. "Who's this?"

"Detective Wallace Friggs of the Cleveland Police Division. We have your client under arrest, and he has requested your presence here."

Keno wiped the sweat from his face. His client list ran from alimony creditors to corrupt politicians. Anyone of them would be in that position.

"Name, please?" He said into the phone, looking for his flip flops.

"Lawrence Ponts, also known as Tunes."

The alias struck a chord in his heart. Tunes was not his client. He was his best friend from high school days. They both peddled marijuana in classrooms, till Tunes got caught and sent to juvenile jail. Keno had a change of direction after that. He took his studies seriously and graduated with distinctions and got into law school.

They had met six months ago, and Tunes jokingly told him that he owed him one, for not snitching on him. And now, it seemed like it was time to return the favor.

"Hello, are you there? The office of the District Attorney will provide a lawyer for him if you decline to see him."

"I'll be there in an hour." Keno severed the connection.

The fuck have you gotten yourself into, Tunes?

When Keno Getty arrived at the precinct, he was met by the detective. He made sure that the room was not wired to record any conversations he will discuss with Tunes, and he walked into the room.

Tunes was quite pleased to see his friend of many years in the room. But his friend, an untidy bulk of a man with a loosely fitting suit and the greasy mark of sweat around his forehead was not exactly pleased to be there.

"Yo Tunes. Did you do all the charges leveled against you?"

"Yes, bruh." And Tunes went on to explain everything in detail.

"This is even worse than I thought, Tunes. Murder. Illegal possession of a firearm. Over speeding. Drug trafficking. Wiggling out of this will be difficult. The most corrupt judge in Cleveland won't be able to swing this in court under the full glare of the jury."

"Fuck!" Tunes cussed. "The detective told me so. He says you ain't gon' be able to help."

"It would seem so. But we still got one more card left to play."

"Which is?"

"We'll be playing right into their hands."

"Talk to me, Keno."

"You'll be placed in protective custody while you release the names and locations of your other gang members."

"I ain't no snitch, man" Tunes barked. "You know this."

"I know this, but the times have changed, Tunes. You ain't going to juvenile prison, bro. I'm talking about the federal pen, bruh. You know the things that happen to people who go to federal pens?"

Tunes shuddered at the thought. "I can't do time, Keno."

"Take whatever deal the police brings your way. It's the only way out of this."

Keno stood up and waved at the plexiglass. The door creaked moments later and Wallace walked in.

"I guess your lawyer has fully debriefed you of the consequences of your actions leading to tonight's fiasco."

"Get on with it, will you?" Tunes said, with a haughty look on his face.

"I will," Wallace said, grabbing a chair from the corner and sat on it. "I like a man who is willing to cooperate."

"Who is in charge of your ring of drug dealing operation?"

"I ain't no snitch." Tunes said.

"Just when I thought you were going to be cooperative." Wallace stood up. "Well, enjoy life in prison. I hear the food is pretty awful."

Keno jostled Tunes, goading him to come clean.

"Mike," Tunes said flatly, staring at the floor.

"Mike what? Mike Tyson? Mike Jackson? Mike Jordan? You gotta be more specific. Help me help you."

"Michael James Gilbert." He said, head bowed in shame.

Wallace raised his index finger in the air, ran it in a circle and brought it down. He was sure someone across had taken down the name and started to run facial recognition.

"And how many of you work for Michael James Gilbert?"

"Seven, including me."

"State all their names for the record."

Tunes was too weak to protest. He did.

"Since your band of drug traffickers is into distribution, who manufactures these drugs?"

"I can't say."

"You can't say, or you won't say?"

"Both, apparently."

"You wanna act smart? From the information you've given to me, I may convince the judge to remove you from solitary confinement, but you'd still be in a federal pen. Start talking."

"I don't know his name. I swear I don't know his name."

"What does he look like?"

"I haven't seen him before."

"What does he go by in the streets?"

"I could be in a lot of trouble for this."

"You, my friend, are already wallowing in deep shit. Out with it."

"King. I only know him as King."

"The King? What sorta name is that?"

"Just King. King is the name."

"Good boy," Wallace heaved a sigh. "We'll let you go, but we're gonna track your every move." He snapped his fingers. The door creaked open and Chloe walked in carrying an ankle bracelet. She placed it on the table and stormed out.

"We have just completed one phase of the arrangement. Now we can begin the second phase."

"No way in hell I'm putting that on me." Tunes protested, eyeing the device with disdain. Keno Getty who had been quiet the whole time tapped him.

"This is standard police protocol, Tunes. You're a CI now."

"A what?"

"Criminal Informant. CI for short."

"A snitch?"

"Yes, Captain Obvious." Wallace rolled his eyes. "Once this is on, I can track your every move. When you go to take a leak at the toilet, I'll know. When you go to the club, I'll know. I'm like Big Brother without the cameras, of course. Before the reality struck on Tunes, Wallace had folded up the jeans of his right leg, and strapped the bracelet in place. Tunes stared in horror as a green light beeped intermittently.

"Just a friendly reminder; this bracelet cannot be removed and it has been calibrated with the map of Ohio. If you ever attempt to leave the state, even so much as an inch out of the boundaries of the state, the green light will turn to red and a jolt of electricity will be sent to your body. So, don't ever think about escaping."

"Fuck!"

"Lastly, you have one week to give us relevant information on how to move on Mike and King. One week."

"The fuck?!"

"I'll be calling you from a secure line to communicate with you. You're our bitch now, so best act like one."

Wallace stood up and made for the door. "Oh, we have fixed the broken plywood wall in your truck. So, your cover won't be blown. Lastly, no one should know about this. I won't divulge into the consequences you'd face if you do." He shut the door behind the two.

"I'm fucked." Tunes said, his eyes watery.

"Yes, bruh" Keno replied patting him on the back. "You're fucked

<u>Chapter Five: Bad Habits.</u>

Tunes was well outside the precinct when his phone rang. He looked at the caller and suppressed the urge to smash the phone on a wall. He gained control of himself and hit the answer button.

"Yo, Ty," He said.

"Nigga, where the fuck you been, man? Debbie's been shot in the streets. There's fucking police all about the area, and you drive off without telling us. The fuck man?"

"The truck broke down," He lied. "I had to fix it up. Meet me at Mike's by noon."

"For sho!" Ty hung the line. Tunes got into his truck, shut the door and started yelled in a fit of rage. He was a snitch now. That was what he never wanted to do from the get-go. He looked at the ankle with glow, and gave a resigned sigh.

He started the truck and jetted off to the opposite direction to his house.

The truck pulled up in the driveway and he got out. For some reason, he just stood outside the driveway and stared at the enveloping darkness that is the night sky. There were no stars tonight, and soon the darkness will be swept away for sunlight.

He stood there a depressed man. Battered. Shattered. Weak.

**

Over 50 miles away from the neighborhood where Tunes lived, a large mansion stood out in the darkness. In its well-guarded walls, a figure waltzed in the dark. As it moved with purpose, the night garment that covered its skin billowed and swirled.

He moved to the large desk and sat down and grabbed one of the twelve sophisticated landlines on the desk and dialed a number. It made for a circular device on the desk and placed it on his mouth. The call rerouted through a secure line. After several clicks, it was answered at the other end.

"Mike, this is King." The figure said. It sounded automated.

"Yo, King, I've bee—"

"A shipment has been transferred to the warehouse on 80th and Detroit. You can pick it up on Friday evening by 9pm."

The one called King severed the connection before the man at the other end ever got the chance to respond in the affirmative. He removed the device from his mouth and placed it on the table. King stood up and grabbed a wine bottle from the cabinet plopped by the side of the office and poured the drink, and sat back down.

King heaved a sigh. Everything was falling in place. Like a pack of cards. Deception is king.

I am deception, the voice spoke.

***

The blonde lady on Mike's television was chatting animatedly as she faced the screen. Mike sat at the lounge and busied himself counting a long stack of huge dollar bills. The volume on the TV was at the lowest, but his ears could pick up what the blonde lady was saying.

"Mr. Mayor," He heard the voice say, and he looked up from the table. The lady was now facing the someone else sitting beside her.

It was the Mayor of Seven Hills alright. It was Roberto Ricci.

"What's your say on the alarming rate at which cases of overdoses of the fentanyl-based drugs have infested the city?"

The Mayor beamed at the presenter, cleared his throat and spoke, his voice had an elegance.

"Well, Jennifer, my press secretary showed me the numbers last week, and I want to place it on record here that I'm perplexed. The fact that people push, sell and buy these drugs knowing fully well how dangerous it is, is a point of concern for me and City Hall."

"Mr. Mayor, there are reports that your administration is somewhat…" The presenter paused to gather her stream of thoughts. "frail towards the fight against drug abuse."

Mr. Mayor laughed. "Jennifer Corbis, trust me those reports are false in all entirety. One thing we should know is that Ohio and America at large are run by a democratic system aimed to better the lives of the people. For a fact, I can say that City Hall is committed to eradicating the ailing issues in the community. Some people think we sit in our big chairs and do nothing. That is so wrong. Thing is, at the end of the day we'll go back to our families, our neighbors and friends. I've got two daughters, and I wouldn't want harm to come their way. We're all a single unit. I have been having meetings with councilmen and women, the DA and police chiefs. We've made some progress in that aspect."

The Mayor lifted his gaze from the reporter and faced the camera. "I guarantee you, Ohioans. We will bring the bad guys to book."

"Like hell, you will," Mike cussed and turned off the TV. As though timed down to seconds, the doorbell rang. Mike stood up, grabbed his firearm under the table and moved to the window that was close to the door. He parted the curtains and when he saw who was standing at the doorpost, he sighed and opened the door.

Tunes walked him, shook his hands and reclined on one of the sofas. He was wearing a polo shirt and jeans pants that seemed to conceal the ankle bracelet strapped in his right foot. It was the right thing to do.

Mike would shoot him point blank if he found that he was wearing a police ankle tracker.

Shortly after, the others arrived and the sound of a loud chatter filled the room.

"Has the police cleared the scene where Debbie died?" Mike asked

"I think so." Ty said. "What's the matter, bruh?"

"I got a shipment from King to pick up on Friday at 9pm."

"King gon' be there?" Tunes asked and shifted uneasily in his seat. Mike eyed him squarely. He could place it, but there was something off about the movements. He was wearing a jeans pants, for one. Tunes loved wearing shorts. But he brushed the thought aside.

Maybe it was the cold from last night, he thought.

"King never shows up. I dunno who the fuck he is, nigga. He could be sitting across from me eating burgers, and I won't know shit. But as long as he gives us the shipment, and we make mo' money off him, we good, right?"

"Right," They all chorused.

Their chatter was interrupted when Tunes' phone rang. When he saw the private number, he excused himself, took the short walk to the bathroom and shut the door behind.

"What the fuck, man?" He whispered into his cellphone.

"What's your status on Mike and King?" Detective Wallace's voice was gruff.

"I dunno, man." Tunes said, scratching his head.

"You know," Wallace's voice carried a casual tone. "I could remotely change the green light on the tracker on your legs to red, and fry you right there. Think I'm joking? Check the bracelet,"

Tunes reached down and raised the fabric upwards, and stared horrifyingly as the green light beeped and change to red. He prepared himself for the shock that will crash through his body. But the light changed back to green.

"You're no use to me paralyzed. Now start talking."

"Mike will be picking up a shipment from King on Friday, 9pm."

"Location?"

"80th and Detroit. The red house at the spot where the junkie bitch died."

"Will King be there?"

"No."

"See? I like it when you cooperate. You're a good sport."

The line severed after that. Tunes gave a defeated sigh and ran the tap on the sink. As the water sluiced out, he poured it on his face.

"Fuck." He muttered.

***

Sergeant Benjamin Winbush's office at the Cleveland Police Department was located at the top of the building. It was a large room, designed to make whoever used was comfortable.

It was in this space that he kept the official records that had been assigned to him in a wooden shelf. Since he was made Captain of Police, he had taken time off real police work and dealt with paperwork. He didn't like the idea, but his team of officers serving under him did their jobs will diligence and this made him to relax.

He, unlike most officers at the station, was a worker, barely taking off time when there was an emergency on his table. That evening, he found himself in the office looking through sheaves of papers that had been brought for his inspection on the mud scandal that had rocked the city he oversaw.

A knock came on the door and the person who had knocked came in, not waiting for a reply for him. Detective Wallace had only made the necessary courtesy out of instinct, both of them knew that the situation they were in demand that their mind is occupied with better things than who knocked or didn't. Wallace was certain that he had read a reasonable amount of the document.

"We've got a lead on Mike," He said as he walked in. "He will be at 80th and Detroit at 9pm to pick up a shipment—possibly mud and fire from King."

"Great news. Will King be there?"

"Negative. We tried to run a facial recognition, but there were not enough leads for the tech team to work with."

"This King is proving to be a real pain in the ass."

"Sure. When we get Mike, he'll lead us to King and we can wrap this thing up."

"Good. Good." Winbush said. "I'll let the Mayor and Councilwoman Sara Jackson know what's happening. They have been on my ass all day."

"Sucks to be you." Wallace joked. The Police Captain took it lightly, chuckling.

"I'll radio the SWAT team to work with you on the stakeout."

"Copy that, boss," Wallace said as he retreated to the door. The meeting was over.

Friday. 80th and Detroit. 7:45pm.

The two unmarked vans eased to a stop five blocks away from the red house. The doors slid open almost immediately and policemen dressed in black uniforms with bulletproof vest stepped out.

Detective Wallace got out eventually and signaled the boys over.

"Alpha team, with me, we go through the front. No force. No pressure. Beta team, you rendezvous at the rear and cover any escape from that point. We sit and wait for the bastard to show up and we take him in. Lethal force is strictly forbidden. Go!"

The men marched expertly and covered the house. The beta team hurried to the back and took positions behind the shed.

"In position," The officer in charge of the beta team said into his walkie

"Roger that," Wallace replied. He signaled his own team, and they got into the house.

***

7:50pm.

Councilwoman Sara Jackson smiled wistfully as she replaced the receiver on her large desk. Sara looked ravishingly young for a woman who was about to hit fifty in a couple of months. She had sharp features, wizened blue eyes which accentuated her light skin. She had a mole on her face just above her upper lip. She was a force to be reckoned with in and out of the state of Ohio.

Reports were making the rounds that she may run for US Senate, but she debunked the news.

"I just want to be close to my people as possible as I can, and give back to the community." She had said. It was regarded as the most noble thing any politician would say.

Every success has a story, and for Sara Jackson, it wasn't painted in bright dazzling colors. Sara had gone through mental issues since she was a child, but she never allowed it to weigh her down. She fought against the odds and has now become a role model for young girls who were aspiring to one day become a politician.

She stood up and walked to the wine chamber, her hips swaying from side to side. She poured herself a drink.

The police were making a lot of progress in the fight against drugs. She had just finished talking to Sergeant Benjamin Wallace, Future captain of the PD in Cleveland, who filled her in about it.

It was great news. Very soon, King will be brought to justice, he had assured her. She had promised to make the motion for a rise in police officers wages if they arrested King. He had assured her that it wasn't necessary, but she had insisted and disconnected the call abruptly.

A morose smile hung on her lips as she raised the glass. "Cheers to the police."

***

8:13pm.

Tunes watched as Creed stepped on the stage and started performing at the gig he had invited the boys. Tunes, Ty, Dilla, O and Tat joined the crowd to cheer him on as he rapped:

"Still new like the shit from the south side

And even when I'm laid on my back, I never back down

It's poker time and I'm the real deal

Fuck with me, bad homie this is Kill Bill.

My flow is like what happens when a sinner praise

Haters seem to be stuck in a beginner stage

They'll soon get the feeling of when a dreamer wakes

While I be gettin' all da shit that a winner takes

Cuz I'm the realest nigga ever made

They need me need me like the better days

I'm about to go off like a dynamite

I'm not an offering, but you can tell a nigga tithe."

The crowd seemed to be feeling him, as their voices raised a fevered pitch. Creed was at one with himself. Dilla excused himself, and went to the men's bathroom. Tat was grinding with a lady he had met on the dance floor. Tunes retreated to the bar section to place an ordered for beer. As he sat and watched, his eyes caught the gorgeous figures of two ladies wearing skimping dresses who had just entered the club. His eyes settled on them, and realization struck his face. He knew one of them.

"Aurora!" He called out. One of the ladies turned to the sound, and seeing him, grabbed her companion and rushed to meet Tunes.

"Lawrence," She screamed, hugging him tightly. "It's been what? Seven years!"

"I go by Tunes now," Tunes said, holding her face. "And yes, I missed you too."

Aurora chuckled. She grabbed her friend by the hands, and facing Tunes she said.

"Lawrence—Tunes meet Samantha. Samantha, Tunes."

"Pleased to meet you," Samantha said.

"The pleasure is mine." Tunes smiled. He loved how rich kids behaved. Friendly. Naïve. Aurora was the daughter of the Mayor of Seven Hills, Roberto Ricci, and they had been friends right from high school until he went to juvenile prison.

"Whatchu doing out here?" He asked the two.

"We came to watch Creed perform, you know, support our own," Aurora said, staring into the distance towards Creed who seemed to be feeding the crowd from his mic.

"And," Samantha dropped her voice to a faint whisper. "we came to score some fire."

Both ladies giggled, and even when they saw the shocked look on his face, they giggled even more.

"Well, I may have what you need," Tunes said. He looked around if anyone was watching. Satisfied that no one was, he fished inside his pocket and brought out two wraps of fire and hand it to them.

"You don't have to pay for it, and please, do not OD."

"You're such a darling," Samantha said, keeping her portion of fire inside her small purse.

Before they left him, the ladies exchanged numbers with him, and joined the crowd dancing and screaming as the Creed rapped.

Tunes felt the need to go the men's bathroom to unload his bowels. The smell of urine and beer crinkled his nostrils. He was feeling nauseated.

Thankfully, one of the booths was free. Tunes jumped in, shut the door, unzipped his fly, and as the hot urine flew out of his member, he was hearing some sort of noise from the next booth.

Leaning closer to the wall that divided both booths, Tunes strained his ears. The voice sounded vaguely familiar. He couldn't place it yet. As Tunes made to zip back his fly, his ears picked up something that made him freeze.

"I understand that this is standard police protocol. Tunes, O, Tat and myself are at a club downtown. Creed is on stage. I can attest that he's free. I will be at the precinct tomorrow."

What the fuck?!

Tunes waited as he heard the flushing sound from the next booth.

He stood still as the figure walked past his booth. His door was skewed to a rather eccentric angle, and the figure that walked past his booth.

The shock registered on Tunes' face.

It was Dilla!

***

8:33pm

"You're no fun," Draper said as he swung the sedan a slow left and cruised on the freeway. Mike, who was riding shotgun with him laughed.

"The ladies beg to differ," Mike said. "They know I got money, and some good D to ease the stress of the day away."

"You wish," Draper said and dodged a playful punch Mike threw his way.

"Watch it, bruh." He yelled. "I'm driving."

"Slow driving ass bitch."

"Fuck you, man,"

"Is that how you ride your chick at home? Her sex life must be very boring."

"Shut the fuck up, man" Draper rolled his eyes. He took a sharp right and 80th and Detroit came into view. Mike's phone began to ring, and when he saw the caller, he quickly hit the answer button and brought the device to his ears.

"I want us to arrange a meet tonight." The voice was unmistakably King's.

"I'm on my way to pick up the shipment," Mike said, motioning Draper to slow down.

"That can wait." The voice said. "Send one of your boys to grab the shipment while you come to meet me at The Baptist Church."

"Did you say The Baptist Church?"

"Guess you heard me correctly." The line went dead. Mike blinked at the screen. He tapped Draper. "Swing the car around."

"Wh—"

"The Baptist Church," Mike said hurriedly, smiling. "We're going to meet King there."

Draper hit the brakes, lurched the car around and jetted off.

***

8:52pm

Mileana was just outside the nightclub, about to go in when her phone vibrated and rang. She fished through her purse and after searching for a couple of seconds, she found the phone and answered the call.

"Yo, Mike." She said.

"Mileana!" She heard Mike heave a sigh of relief. "Thank god, you answered."

"What's the problem, babes?"

"I need you to go pick up the shipment at 80th and Detroit. I've been calling the boys, and they ain't picking up. I got someplace to be. Can you handle it?"

"Forsho!" Mileana smiled. She had been waiting for an

opportunity like this, and seeing that it presented itself, now wasn't a time to disappoint Mike. "I'll get in my ride now."

She disconnected the line and ran back into her car.

***

9:09pm

Mileana switched the gears of her sedan, the car grumbled and increased pace on the less-busy traffic. She stared briefly at the youngsta riding shotgun with her. It was her kid brother, Slim.

She had picked him up on the way from basketball practice. His eyes were fixed on his phone, watching several YouTube videos of LeBron James playing basketball. He wanted to one day become like him. She believed in his dream, and that was the reason most of her earnings from the drug trade went into private basketball sessions. Scouts usually flock to these places to watch young players practice, and she wanted Slim to be there when they did.

"Milli, what are you making for dinner?" He asked, his eyes still glued to the phone.

"Nigga, you're a grown ass man," She replied, rolling her eyes. "You cook your own food now."

"I don't think LeBron cooks his own food," He muttered under his breath.

"Watchu say?"

"I said LeBron looks so good in purple too."

"Idiot."

She swung the car into 80th and Detroit, zoomed past the unmarked vans parked at the corner of the street, sped a few blocks and ground to a halt in front of a red house.

"Wait for me here," She said to Slim, as she slid out of the car.

"No freakin' way, Mili."

"I just wanna grab somethin' and I will be back."

"I'm a grown ass man, remember?" Slim jumped out of the car and joined her at the sidewalk. "Let me help you carry your whatever it is, and then you can make me dinner when we get home,"

"Sneaky little bastard." Mileana couldn't help but smile at the lanky frame of her kid brother. They both took the flight of stairs to the house.

If they had been listening carefully, their ears would've picked up movements of on a patch of grass just behind the building.

It was Slim who knocked at the door, and waited for a response. When they heard none, Mileana rapped the doors. They weren't hearing any movements approaching the door. Slim thought he heard shifting noises, but he brushed it aside. Endless basketball sessions did that to him. He heard scribbling noises when they were none.

Time slowed as Mileana reached to turn the knob of the door, and it swung open.

It was dark inside.

***

9:15pm

Draper pulled up the car as the towering building of The Baptist Church swarm into focus. It was a rectangular edifice that ran straight up some feet and caved into the center in a fine triangle. A huge white cross stood at the head of the church but there had been no messiah on it. It bore the mark of the many sinners who had come into its belly to pour out the filth of their souls. It looked poorly kept and anemic.

"I can't believe we have to come here to do business. Nothing is sacred, eh?" Draper said as he turned off the ignition.

"Money is the only sacred thing I know," Mike replied, a smirk plastered on his lips. "And in there, is what will make me more money." His eyes traveled through the area, scanning for any strange movements. There was no one in sight. As he scanned the building again, a small jerking caught his peripheral focus. He noticed that it was a light from the window inside the building. It was coming from a small torch, figured. It flickered on and off intermittently.

Mike nudged Draper, and showed him the flickering light. "I guess that's the signal."

"Guess it is."

"Keep the car running, bruh. From my few convos with him, I don't think the man is a typa dude that like to be kept waiting."

Mike pushed the door open, stepped out and made a beeline for the church's front entrance. Draper put the car into a slow ride and it glided smoothly out of view just as the other car was coming from the other end. The car performed the same process almost ritually.

He drew out a cigarette and lit it. He puffed out the thick smoke. It was comforting to know that if anything went awry, he would be taking his leave inside a church.

The double doors of the church made an eerie sound as they opened and shut behind him.

He hadn't perceived the two men who stood quietly behind the door when he entered, and he was too slow to react when they grabbed him. They held him with a forcefulness from behind before he could reach for his weapon and frisked him down. They took the weapon that he had snuck up his hips, and the penknife he'd kept on his boots.

The fuck is this?

He was here to do business and he was being handled like a common thief? The man on his right grunted at him when the frisking was done. He motioned for Mike to go on down the aisle.

"Proceed," One of them said, his hands stretching forward. "The priest will take your confessions."

Mike moved down the aisle to the altar, took a left and started towards the door. As he moved, he saw a handful of other men that took positions on the pews that lined the aisle. He felt like a sitting duck with so much eyes that peered at him. Although no one had made a sudden move at him, and the moment, he felt like it was a good thing.

He entered the booth and shut the door behind him. He moved toward the only seat in the confession box and pressed his weight on it. He heard movements from the clerical side of booth. As if on cue, a small hole slid open. It was too dark for his eyes to see anything.

Mike cleared his throat. It was his way of breaking the ice. When the person at the other end wasn't responsive, he wiped his face and spoke.

"Forgive me father, for I have sinned?"

"Save your breath, Mike. We're going to hell." The voice said. Mike noted it that it was somewhat automated. Like whoever it was, was speaking to a device that transmitted what he was hearing. "Were you followed here?"

"I don't think so," Mike faltered.

"You're a very bright boy, Mike, and I love how you've managed to build yourself an empire out of my hands."

Mike shifted in his seat. He wished he had his firearm with him. What was King going with this?

"I do aight," He said.

"With great power comes great responsibility," King said. "And I've got a great responsibility for you. I have manufactured a new drug. I call it Dog Food."

"Dog food?"

"Not a catchy name, I know. But let's roll with it, okay?"

"Cool." Mike's face brightened up.

"We're gonna make loads of money with this one, trust me. Because this is new and delicate, I'm going to be in charge of the operations myself. You are to arrive at the Cleveland Port docks on Tuesday 9pm to pick up the new shipment. I've got a thing with 9pms. Come alone and don't be followed."

"Cool!"

"Oh, and before I forget. You have a mole in your house."

Mike shook his head. "King, I've got mad respect for you, but i—"

"The police are turning ranks inside your house. You'll find out soon enough."

"No fucking way I'm gon' believe that."

"Best believe that. This meeting is over. In fact, it never existed. Go on, your sins are forgiven."

Mike heard the metallic click of the hole sliding shut. Mike stood up, and rushed to the main auditorium. There was no one standing by the entrance doors, or seated in the pews. As he paced down the aisle, an object glinted in the pew closest to the double entrance doors.

It was his pen knife, he realized when he closed the distance. His firearm was sitting beside it. He grabbed both weapons and stumbled out of the church.

"Woo. That was quick," Draper remarked, as Mike slid into the car. He had expected a joke or a comeback from Mike, but he only muttered the words, "Just drive."

Draper tried to search his face, but Mike had gambler's eyes. Expressionless. Emotionless. With a defeated sigh, Draper switched gears and jerked the car forward.

***

9:19pm.

Mileana's fingers ran through the wall, till she found the light switch.

Nothing prepared her for what happened next.

It happened in split seconds. She caught a movement from the corner of her eyes, and before her brain could process what she had seen, a shot fired off. She felt a perpetual sting just below her abdomen as the bones around the flesh rattled. The momentum pulled her backwards.

She crashed into the wall behind her. In the dizzying moments that followed, she heard two more shots; another bullet had found its way into her chest. As her frame hit the ground, her eyes flew to see her brother clutching his chest and stumbling to the ground.

No. This is not happening. This is a nightmare!

She willed herself to grab him, but her body never moved.

The last thing she saw as darkness enveloped her was a man rushing to her side, and screaming "Noooo!"

"Fuck!" Wallace screamed as he checked her pulse. He couldn't read any pulse. The two bullets were fatal, and they made were fired to kill. There was no use checking the young fellow that lay sprawled beside her.

There was no use at all.

Wallace stood up and with the suddenness of a fired bullet dashed towards the SWAT officer who had fired the shots.

"You stupid fuck!" He punched him across the face. The punch pummeled the officer backwards. "I said no force, no pressure!" He hurled his boot into the stomach of the officer. "I said lethal force is strictly forbidden!" He punctuated his annoyance with another kick. "They were fucking unarmed!"

The other SWAT buddies grabbed Wallace and disengaged him from wrecking another kick to their comrade.

"I'm gonna have your badge and head for this!" Wallace screamed, and stormed out of the building. "At ease, beta team," He spoke into the walkie. "Rally around, grab the shipment, and call an ambulance." He wanted to be anywhere but there. He flagged down an on duty Lyft driver, and when the driver asked for the destination, he thought hard about it.

"Cleveland precinct," He said flatly.

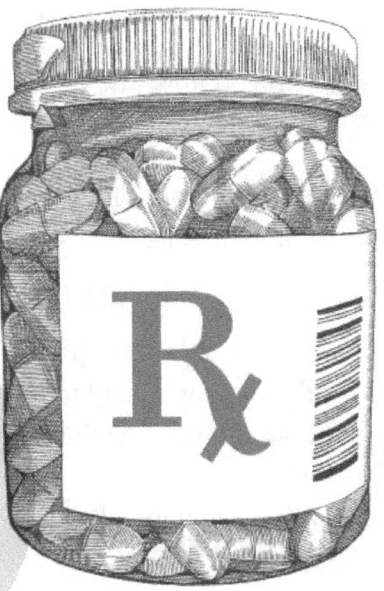

More than **40** PEOPLE die every day from overdoses involving **prescription opioids**.

SHOWTIME

<u>Chapter Six: Showtime</u>

Tunes paced up and down the living room of his apartment, his head a myriad of thoughts.

Everything is spilling out of control. He could tell. He stared briefly at the ankle tracker that was on his leg and cussed.

When he drove the boys home last night after the party at the club, he couldn't take his eyes off Dilla. He just couldn't. He wondered if Dilla was the dude who had tried to kill him. It would make a lot of sense if he was. Dilla was the dude who spoke less in group meetings, avoided conversations like a plague, and no one bothered him because they all felt he was a reserved fella, and that was a good thing.

But mutha fucking mute is a police?! Fuck!

His phone rang, bringing his strides to a halt. He looked at the screen, and groaned as he brought it to his ears.

"You lied to me," Detective Wallace's voice was harsh. "You told us Mike would be there."

"The fuck?" Tunes said. "Mike told us that he'd be there to pick up a shipment."

"But he never showed up. He sent another two members of your crew to pick up the shipment."

"What the—"

"You lied to me."

Tunes heard the sharp tone of the line being disconnected. He cussed, hurling the phone across the sofa.

What made Mike changed his mind? Did Dilla inform Mike?

His train of thoughts was jumbled up and scattered to smithereens. He was still trying to bring calm to his ailing mind when the phone rang again. He saw the caller and a cold ran down his spine.

"Mike," He said, and placed the phone on speaker.

"Mileana and Slim are dead," His voice reverberated through the room, sending shockwaves to his body.

"The fuck?!?!"

"Get to the house. Right now."

***

"We used to be a family, a single unit." Mike was saying, as he faced his band of drug dealers. His hands were deftly clasped around two side arms that were aiming at no one in particular. "I can't trust no one no more."

Niecesa was sobbing on Dilla's shoulder, the tears dripping and soaking his shirt. Tat was trying in vain to console her.

"It could've been me and Draper last night. Now Slim and Milli are lying dead at the morgue. And it's because someone here snitched to the police."

Mike raised his left hand and released fired two shots at the TV in rage. As the hail of glass fell and scattered on the floor, Mike stared them all down as they tried to get up from their seats.

"I made y'all rich overnight, and y'all turn around to stab me in the back?! Get the fuck outta here! Get the fuck outta my house! If you don't hear from me, do not come looking for me. I'll murk ya if you do. Get out!"

Mike held a haughty look on his face as they hurried out of the house.

"Muthafuckas!" He cursed.

***

When Tunes got home that afternoon, there was only one thought that lingered and filled his mind. Escape.

It had gotten really complicated with the police gunning down Mileana and her younger brother, Slim. Guilt overshadowed him, as he ran the water from the sink down his face.

The blasted tracker that sat on his ankle was another reminder that he could be next person that the police would cross off their list. He had cooperated with them every step of the way, and now they've started killing his friends?

He knew he couldn't escape, if he doesn't get electrified to death, first. As the water sluiced down his face, his mind flashed to his juvenile prison days when water per bath was regulated, and he remembered how Madd, his roommate would ask him to hurry with his bath.

That was it!

Madd!

He remembered that Madd was a computer genius, a firewall

expert and a hacker. He remembered that Madd was arrested, for cybercrimes. He had hacked into the servers of CIA, and photocopied the addresses of every CIA safehouses all over the globe. He had planned to sell it to a dealer on the Dark Web, when his IP was tracked down, and he was arrested on several counts of treason. While Tunes remained there, he made sure that no inmate bullied the kid. And they made quite an acquaintance.

He remembered how Madd used to tell him that anything can be bought on the Dark Web—a framework of incognito and heavily encrypted IPs and landing pages. Everything from bitcoin, hard drugs, video games, child porn, sex dolls, hired assassins, and slaves can be bought on the Dark Web.

Of course, it was a crazy thing to say, and Tunes told him so, but Madd only shook his head.

"There are a lot of things in the world that you don't know."

One the night before Tunes was to be released, Madd had written a series of passkeys on a sheet of paper and gave them to Mike and made him promise not to reveal details of it to anyone else.

Mike still had the sheet of paper with him. He had kept it in his top drawer.

I need to get the fuck outta here, and this Dark Web may be the only way.

He made for the top drawer in his bedroom and spilled all the contents on the floor. He ransacked every item till he found the sheet of paper. He blinked at the web address that Madd had written down. It didn't make any sense at all, but there was no harm in trying.

He turned on his laptop and typed the web address into the tap and pressed. A notification beeped that the connection was encrypted and he clicked continue till he got to a landing page.

He stared at the sheet of paper and pressed the keys into a box and pressed the ENTER key. The screen made a sharp tone and it blacked out.

When it came back, the landing pages was different, and he instinctively knew where he was when he sifted through the content.

He was in the Dark Web.

What he saw brought coldness to his feet. Everything Madd whispered to him about the Dark Web in their cell several years ago was true. There were several ads for several purposes.

He quickly punched in Police Ankle Bracelet into the search box. Three results displayed on the screen.

'Buy Police Ankle Bracelet.

Sell Police Ankle Bracelet

Hack Police Ankle Bracelet.'

That was it. He need someone to hack the bracelet, decrypt the machine and free it from his leg. He clicked the last result. A pop-up appeared on the screen, requesting the user to pay $2,000 to proceed. He quickly brought out his credit card punched in some numbers and did the transfer.

The screen blacked out and came up shortly. The screen was black, save for the username of someone that had sent him a message.

What do you need?

Tunes typed in a reply. 'I want to get this tracker off my ankle.' The response came in seconds.

Show me.

Tunes did a snapshot of the tracker on his leg, and sent the media file.

This is a P-5453UI4 tracker. Relatively new in the police force. But like the others before it, it can be hacked.'

Tunes threw a fist bump in the air. Yes! His escape plans will come to fruition. He hurriedly typed the next set of keys into the screen. 'How much do you need?'

I don't accept cash.

'What do you accept then? Bitcoin?' Tunes sent. He waited as the unknown person typed.

40 pounds of mud

The fuck? Tunes thought. 'What do you need that amount of mud for?' He sent.

Your freedom, Tunes.

Tunes stumbled backwards. He stared at the screen, bewilderment hanging on his mind. Another message appeared on the screen.

Don't fret. It's me Madd.

Tunes rushed back to the table, and started tying excitedly into the screen.

'Aye, Madd. How did you find out it was me?'

I guess my lectures on encryption in that cold prison cell didn't sink in your skull. You were using your laptop username to chat with me which is quite dangerous. I ran a search and your real name popped up.

'Shit.'

Can you make arrangements for mud?

Tunes did a mental calculation. He had about 70 pounds of mud under his bed, and if he were to make the trade, Mike won't be aware he had escaped till he was well across the Mexican borders, free from US jurisdictions and he would blend with the natives there.

'If I bring it in, how soon can you work on the tracker?'

Today. Noon. I'll send you the address and my number to your cell.

Tunes wondered how he got his cells, but he was too bedazzled to ask. Shortly after, a file was sent. Tunes downloaded and opened it. The address was a house in 108th and Kinsman.

'I'll be there.' Tunes typed into the screen and shut his laptop. He stole a quick glance at the wall clock. It was 11:15am.

Just then, his phone began to ring. He peered at the caller. It was the last person he'd expected to ring his cell.

"Hello, Samantha," He said.

"Hey, Tunes," She spoke. It sounded as though she was weak and inebriated. "I need some mud. Can I come by the house?"

Not when I'm planning my escape, bitch. "Nope. I'm on my way to a friend's."

"Can I come around to meet you there? I really need some mud, puh-lease," He could hear the voice of a little girl crashing around.

"Stella, shut the fuck up. I'm still looking for a good reason your sister asked me to baby sit your ass." He heard Samantha scream to the child.

Fuck. "I'll text you the address," Tunes said and ended the connection. He copied the message he received from Madd and sent it to her. He dashed into his bedroom, packed a few clothes in a backpack and threw it in the trunk of his car outside. He came back inside and grabbed a reasonable amount of mud into the trunk. He was sure it was more than what Madd had requested, but he want to do away with it anyway.

When he got into his car, he had one more loophole to fix.

Dilla. It was the problem that stuck out like a sore thumb. Dilla needs to be ghost before he goes off mouthing to the police.

Tunes thought hard about it. He would pick up Dilla on the way to Madd's. Kill him and dump his body where no one will come looking. Get the tracker hacked and removed and get the fuck out of Cleveland and Ohio.

It was a nice plan.

"Aye Dilla"

"What's good?, Tunes," Dilla replied over the line. "Mike call you yet?"

"Nah, bruh. I wanna grab a bite at a new spot in town. Wanna ride?"

"Forsho. You're on speaker. Creed is here. Kiddo wanna go too?,"

This is going to be difficult, Tunes thought as he turned the ignition of the car, slid it out the driveway in the busy traffic.

Two hours later, Tunes was dead; a neck shot from his own

firearm.

Chapter 7: Flirting with Disaster

Now. 3pm.

The command center of the Cleveland Police Department was filled with men and women smartly dressed in uniforms.

The Governor of Ohio, Antonio Ricci had called Washington in the wake of the recent drug epidemic, but it was evident that it was because of the death of his 9-year old niece, Stella Ricci, that made him order for agents of the FBI and DEA, and now the agents were getting briefed on recent progress that had been made so far.

Surprisingly, SWAT officers were not in the room. Detective Wallace made sure they never showed up.

Sergeant Winbush was placed in a compromising position as he sat beside the agents in the room. FBI agents usually took over tactical operations like this. But this was his turf. They don't know the streets like he and Wallace did.

"We have the names of the drugs dealers," Wallace said, and pointed to the wall which now contained images of the Mike's gang. The faces of Mileana and Tunes had been crossed off. A clipping of Mike's image was at the top of the triangle. Only one

John Doe remained.

King.

"We have their current locations from their cell phones. Their numbers were on the phone of the CI who died today. The numbers were a perfect match with the ones our undercover officer Raymond Dillard supplied us. They may discard it if we don't make any move. From the looks of things, Mike and Draper are in their respective homes. If we take these two, we can proceed to blocking off all the exits of out the city; roadblocks, trains, seaports, you name it. We can get all of these guys tonight. Mike will bring us King."

They all nodded in the affirmative. The plan was rock solid.

They all stood up and dispersed, leaving Winbush and Wallace in the room.

"Has the Mayor called?"

"Is that a trick question? The Governor has my direct cell. He has called a few times."

Winbush's phone began to ring. He grabbed the phone from his pocket, stared briefly at the caller and showed it to Wallace.

It was Councilwoman Sara Jackson. He placed the phone on speaker.

"Hello, ma'am."

"Let's put a raincheck on that meeting."

"What's the matter, ma'am?"

"That information is way above your security clearance...and paygrade. Whereas, I will be coming back to the city on Friday."

Winbush coughed uneasily.

"So, what are your leads so far?" She asked.

Winbush's gaze lingered on Wallace. They stared awkwardly for a couple of minutes.

"Are you still there?" She asked.

"Yes, ma'am," Winbush said. "I was taking a moment to gather my thoughts. Right now, we have no leads on Mike or King. It may seem that they have eluded us yet again." He lied. It was a thing of ego. He wanted to play the-element-of-surprise card at her when they finally brought those criminals to justice.

"Keep me posted." She said and ended the call.

"Ghost Protocol?" Wallace smiled.

"Ghost Protocol," Winbush replied. "Let's keep the media and these politicians guessing. At the end of the day, they all want results, and we will give it to them."

***

"Listen to what I'm about to tell you," Draper said into the phone, as he moved hurriedly through the house. "You gotta get the fuck outta Cleveland, Creed. The clouds are thick, and it's about to rain hard,"

"Where the fuck do you want me to go? I've built a good thing here, man. Are you telling me to leave it all and run away?"

"Nigga, get the fuck outta Cleveland!" Draper screamed and shut his phone.

Time was of the essence here. His mind was a quagmire of uncertainties. In the space of two days, he had lost two of his peeps. Who is next? Not me!

He grabbed whatever he could find, and stacked some cash into the box. Making sure that the bag was properly zipped, he bounded the stairs to the unexpected scene that played out before him.

A handful of semi-autos gaped at him. His eyes roved wildly at the lounge. He was surrounded by men wearing FBI outfits.

"Put your hands in the air, and get on your knees!" One of the agents commanded.

"Any sudden moves, and you'll be shot." Another agent barked.

***

Mike paced around in his living room, oblivious to what was happening around. If only he hadn't shot the only television he kept in his living room, he would've been abreast with recent developments. Most recently, he would've seen the dead body of his crew member, Tunes, being wheeled out of a crime scene.

But his mind was someplace else. His mind was filled with pain.

I gotta deal to score with King on Friday, and I don't even know who the fuck to trust!

He stood up and slammed his fist into a wall, the ensuing pain wracking through his arms. As he made to enter the bathroom to wash his bloodied fist, a movement from the window caught his attention.

It was fast, but his brain could process what he'd seen. Three men dressed in full body armor with DEA inscribed on the chest region were outside his house.

Fuck!

He grabbed his firearm and fired two shots in quick succession. The bullets flew and grazed the shoulder blade of one of the DEA agent, the corresponding momentum pushed him backward.

Mike raced through the lounge, into the kitchen and out the back door and started running.

"Shots fired! I repeat shots fired! Officer down. Not fatal but request evac. Suspect is armed and on the loose. We're going after him!"

Mike ran as fast as his feet could carry him. He jumped over a hedge, breaking his sprint and propelled his body to move. When he turned, he noticed that the agents were shortly behind. They had a clear line of sight to have put him down, Mike figured. But they haven't shot him. The reality of that struck a chord in his head.

They want me alive.

He lurched into a barbeque party that was holding out in the lawn of beside a building, pushed a couple of people standing in his path into the mini swimming pool, jumped over the wooden fence and landed to the ground.

His eyes looked ahead; he noticed that he was standing at the sidewalk of a road. His mind was too tired to come to terms with which street he was on. He noticed that he still had his firearm on him. Throwing caution to the wind, he shucked the weapon on a patch of grass, and started running. Adrenaline pumped through his body, as his heart pounded in erratic heaves.

There was not going to be any deal with King!

He took another hard left and he saw a Lyft taxi light shine bright and he hurried to the car. He grabbed the door and jumped in the backseat. His gun was exposed in the driver vision.

"Drive!" He barked to the driver.

"Huh, Where?" The driver asked frightenedly.

"Just get me the fuck outta here!"

"Actually, you're going nowhere." Mike heard another voice. It was then that he realized that there was someone riding shotgun with the driver. He wasn't thinking when he jumped in. They must've commandeered the Lyft taxi, and now he had fallen right into their hands.

Outside, a couple of DEA agents were coming towards the Lyft taxi.

Escape was impossible.

***

Ty and O were at the bar when the breaking news of KNTV streamed on the screen. They saw their friend Tunes and the daughter of the Mayor being wheeled into an ambulance, and they instinctively knew that the Cleveland wasn't the best place to be.

Cleveland wasn't safe.

They vaulted over the counter and stumbled out the door, against the club manager's protests. They got into the Chevy and swung the car into the highway. Ty floored the pedal, and the car breezed forward speeding past the motorcade.

"Been tryna call Draper. My network is messed up." O said, tapping irritably at the screen.

Ty stole a quick glance at his phone resting on the panel. "My network's out too, man. Dunno what the fuck is happening. Best we throw the phones away." And with that, he threw his device out the window. He heard the thud.

O contemplated discarding his device. As the thought lingered in his head, Ty snatched the device from his grasps and threw it out of the window.

It was a moment he had taken his eyes off the road. When his eyes returned to the road, it was too late.

"Aye, watch o—"

O's words were clamped back as the impact of the truck which had rammed into them when Ty was briefly distracted pummeled him backward. His head slammed into the headrest and raw unadulterated pain coursed through him.

The airbags exploded on their faces, and knocked them out unconscious.

***

Detective Wallace Friggs led a small team of policemen out of a nondescript van into the evening sun. He walked quickly, with efficiency and purpose in their gait. Pedestrians who were at the sidewalk hurried out of the way as they swept past. They rounded up at the corner.

Wallace raised two fingers in the air and pointed at the rear of the house. They understood. Two men nodded and as they made to cover the rear, a gunfire rang out. The sound emanated from the house.

"Move!" Wallace barked.

The men got in position behind him, and ran to the house. Wallace raised three fingers in the air, and counted down to one. A quick nod of his head was the signal the officer behind him needed. He swung his leg and brought it down against the door. The force blew the door apart. Wallace got in, swinging his weapon, sweeping everywhere he looked.

He dropped his weapon when he saw the bizarre image before him on the ground. He grabbed his walkie from his hip and spoke into it.

"The one called Tat shot himself. He's dead. How's it going over there?"

"We got Draper and Mike."

"The bartenders?"

"Knocked out cold. They were trying to escape when a drunk truck driver ran into them. They're both resting in the ICU with handcuffs strapped to their bed."

"Copy that." Wallace ended the connection.

***

Niecesa stared at the TV special that was transmitting the images of Tunes and Stella Ricci into the ambulance, and a sudden dread crept up her spine.

What the fuck is happening?!

She sat on the sofa, and threw a blanket over her shivering frame. She wasn't over the death of Mileana and Slim, and now Tunes? Niecesa lived alone, save for times when Mike came over to fuck. He wasn't exactly good in bed, but it never bothered her. As long as she had a man in her life, she was fine with it.

But now, everything was spiraling out of control. She knew it. She was too broken to do anything with it. She resigned to fate as she sat on her couch, and stared vacantly at nothing in particular.

And even when the cops came shortly after, she didn't resist the arrest; she held up her hands as they placed the handcuffs on her. She was too tired to fight.

<u>Chapter Eight: Rock N' Roll</u>

Interrogation Room, Cleveland Precinct.

"Michael James Gilbert," Detective Wallace Friggs approached the perp with slow, measured steps. "A man who would rather be called Mike. Let's see what we have here." He opened a dossier containing Mike's face.

Mike sat in one of the chairs, handcuffed to the table. His body throbbed with a numbing pain, the result of sprinting several blocks evading police arrest until he was caught. Just because he was sloppy.

"You were placed in a relief home after your mother died. But you escaped, and no one heard from you till now.

Your right-hand man, Draper has told us everything. All the spots you covered in your drug trade; the laundromats, the theaters, the exotic clubs and bars, and everywhere else. And we've got everything to put you in prison for lif—"

"Who snitched on me?" Mike reeled out in outburst. "I just wanna know."

"You're in no position to make any request." Wallace said calmly. "Right now, you've got one job description; comply to everything we say."

"Who snitched on me?"

Wallace was in a tough spot. He could feel his control slowly drifting away to the perp before him. He had pressed to have the first 'go' at him when the DEA had brought him, while they questioned the others. And now the moment was intense; he knew if he didn't make this guy start talking, the federal agents who were watching behind the glass would take over the whole thing.

I'm not gonna let that happen.

"Let's make a deal, shall we?" Wallace said, and sat down faced the perp. "You tell me what I want to hear, I tell you what you want to hear."

Their gaze lingered for a couple of seconds, and it seems as though it was a staring down contest. Wallace was good at this. It was another psychology thing he'd picked up in Police Academy several years ago.

Mike's eyes twitched after a while and he blinked, looking away.

"Who's King?" Wallace asked.

"I dunno what you talkin' about." Mike replied.

"Don't play dumb with me. Draper said both of you drove to meet him at The Baptist Church,"

"The fuck. Nigga snitched on me?"

"I ask the questions, Mike. I'll answer yours when you answer mine. Who's King?"

"We didn't see eye-to-eye, man."

"What do you mean?"

"He was perched on the priest side of the confession box. Didn't see his face. Nigga was speaking through a device."

Mike raised his fingers. He'd hoped the guys in the box understood his signal to mean that he wanted the place checked out. Chloe would understand. Unfortunately, she wasn't granted access to the viewing room.

"What do you mean through a device?"

"Shit felt like he was speaking through something."

"What did both of you talk about?"

"About some new drugs, he wants me to push."

"Some new drugs?"

"He said it was gonna be hot when it hit the streets."

Wallace smiled. He was making progress. "Name of this drug?"

"He called it Dog Food."

"And he wants you to push it? This Dog Food?"

"Yes."

"When and where are you supposed to make the drop?"

Mike looked at the officer and saw the concern in his eyes. It was as if they shared a psychic connection. Mike knew that the information mattered to him. To him, it was loyalty and if there was anything he really wanted to find out, he wanted to know who was disloyal in his single unit.

"Cleveland Port. Tuesday. 9pm. Now, who the fuck snitched on me?"

Wallace was already jumping to the door. "Tunes! But he's dead."

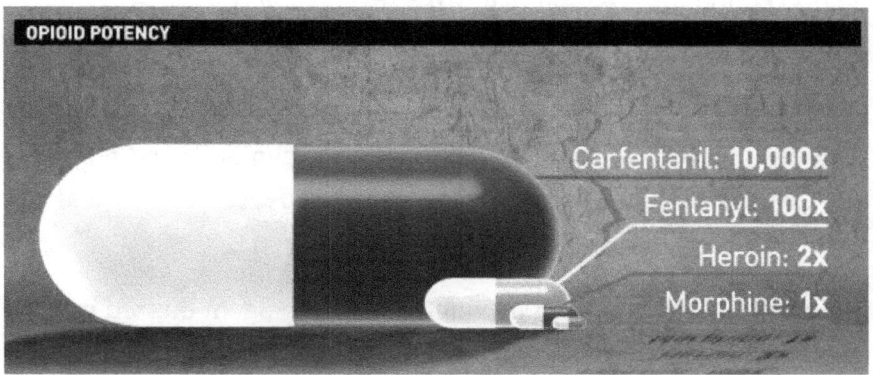

Carfentanil- (King's new drug "Dog Food") is an analogue of the synthetic **opioid analgesic** fentanyl. It is one of the most **potent** opioids known. Its potency is approximately 10,000 times stronger than **morphine** and 100 times stronger than fentanyl. It is a general anesthetic designed for large animals. DANGEROUS!!!

***

Port of Cleveland. 8:45pm.

The night sky shone brightly and glinted in the waters as it lapped gently towards its tributaries. The terrain around Lake Erie was quiet, save for the incessant buzzing of flies that swept pass.

"How long do we have to stay here?" One of the agents buzzed into his coms. He was wearing a branded FBI shirt.

"As long as it takes." Another agent replied.

A team of ten stayed hidden from a vantage point, and watched the entrance of the freight shipping port; they were led by Wallace Friggs. Another team covered the I-71 highway south to

Strongsville and Cincinnati. A tactical assault team covered the I-90 highway east to Willoughby and west to Toledo.

As Wallace's binoculars scanned the port for the umpteenth time, he prayed the information that Mike revealed was legit. After the interrogation with Mike, a tech team had analyzed the videotape with their machines and confirmed that it was the truth.

And now he was waiting to take this King down once and for all, and go back home, satisfied that he had the streets were once again free.

"I detect movements from the south side," An agent buzzed into his ear. He grabbed his binoculars and gleaned through. He zoomed on the location. Three SUVs were driving into the port through the south entrance.

"C'mon, let's go take a closer look."

The team slinked down from where they were and moved slowly but efficiently. They rolled under a cargo and hid there. The SUVs ground into a halt. The doors flew open and heavily armed men stepped out and walked smartly to the SUV in the middle. One of them opened the doors, and a figure stepped out. He tried to zoom in but it was difficult.

"What's the time?" He heard a voice say in monotone. It was remotely familiar to what Mike spoke about in the interrogation room.

"8:58, boss."

"Perfect. Let's wait for Mike to arrive, eh?"

That was it. That was King.

"On my count," Wallace spoke softly into the walkie, Wallace waited for them to start moving, and muttered go!

The men rolled out of the cargo and with assault rifles aimed at them, Wallace screamed.

"FREEZE!"

The men suddenly broke their strides.

"This is the Cleveland PD," Wallace said.

"And the DEA," someone said behind him

"And the FBI," another spoke.

"And you're under arrest. Drop your weapons and put your hands where we can see them."

Out in the open, Wallace could see them clearly. They outnumbered them, but they had the element of surprise. The one he figured was wearing a black mask over his face. A sophisticated circular object sat where his mouth should be.

This was King!

"Not gonna happen," The one with the metallic voice said. "Fire!" He yelled and started towards a section of cargo ships.

The whole terrain exploded in gunfire. Wallace ducked and rolled to the side and started heading for the retreating figure. A bullet brushed his ear making him break his sprints. He recoiled, aimed his firearm and squeezed a set of double taps. The bullets slammed into the man's head and throat, splattering pieces of brain tissues and bones on the tarmac.

He looked up ahead; the figure was had step into a speedboat, and was fiddling with the keys to unlock the door. The distance was too far between them was too far for him to catch up.

Wallace raised his weapon, leveled it, and squeezed a round.

The bullet hit King in the arm, throwing the bunch of keys into the water. Wallace sprinted over like his life depended on it.

"Surrender!" He barked, his weapon aiming the back of his head.

King turned to face him. "Or what?" its mechanical voice said.

King raised both his arms in the air as though in a surrender, and in a split second, pulled the mask off his own face.

The blonde hair fell freely to the side.

Wallace gasped and his face went pale in horror.

Councilwoman Sara Jackson was blinking back at him.

"What do you wanna do? Arrest me?"

"You're a crimi—"

"I won't even spend a month in jail. I'll make some calls, blackmail some people in DC, and I'll be out before you know it. And I'll come for you, your wife and you—"

Two successive shots rang out and drowned her words. Her hands flew to clutch her chest. Wallace noticed that crimson was oozing seeping through her palms. She coughed and fell to the floor of the speedboat.

Wallace stared at his jittering hands. I never pulled the trigger.

"I saved you the worry of ending her," A man called from the back. Wallace turned to see an FBI agent walking towards him. "You heard her. She was planning to blackmail someone in DC. I work for DC. I can't let that happen. Besides, I just scanned the boat with my binoculars. There's a truckload of a substance in there."

It was that moment that Wallace noticed that the gunfire had dissipated.

Wallace walked over the dead councilwoman and peered through the glass. Stacked from the ground to the top of the boat was a white substance with the emblem of a happy Chihuahua.

Dog Food.

Wallace grabbed his phone and called his boss. It rang for a couple of seconds and Winbush raspy voice came on the line.

"Tell me you got good news."

"Yes," He replied. "King is Councilwoman Jackson,"

"My God!"

"She's dead. No loose ends."

"Good job, Wallace. Ghost Protocol has been disengaged. Lemme call the Mayor."

***

Creed was at his parent's apartment when the cops came for him. Officer Raymond Dillard knocked on the door. When Creed opened the door, and saw the cop standing before him, a cold rush ran down his spine.

"Ray Dilla!" He screamed.

"Officer Raymond Dillard," Dilla said. "You're under arrest for the murders of Stella Ricci and Lawrence Ponts who you know as Tunes," and Dilla read him his Miranda rights and handcuffed him.

"You were an undercover cop?"

"You got that right. I was slowing building up a case against Mike all these years. I have to bring you in to testify, and to swing the Jury's decision against you. I know you didn't kill them intentionally. I was there, remember? C'mon, let's go."

Dilla unclasped the handcuff from his hip and strapped them on Creed's hands.

As Creed was led away from the house into the car, he could hear his mother and girlfriend sobbing inside.

"It's gonna be fine, Creed," Dilla reassured him as he pressed his head lightly into the back of the car.

Dilla slams the car door and shook his head. Dilla's phone is ringing and he hits the answer button. Before he can say hello, a little girl's voice is screaming "daddy help me" in the background then an explosion happens on the other end of the phone.

Dial tone....

THE END